THE VANDAL

THE
VANDAL

ANN SCHLEE

Catnip

CATNIP BOOKS
Published by Catnip Publishing Ltd
14 Greville Street
London EC1N 8SB

First published 1979 by Macmillan Children's Books
This edition published 2012

1 3 5 7 9 10 8 6 4 2

Text copyright © Ann Schlee, 1979

The moral rights of the author have been asserted.

A CIP catalogue record for this book is available from the British Library.

ISBN 978-1-84647-138-4

Printed in India by Replika Press

www.catnippublishing.co.uk

With love to Kris

CHAPTER ONE

THE FIRST OUTBREAK of vandalism occurred the week of the University Entrance Examinations, a fact made much of by the psychiatrist at the Special Investigations Clinic where Paul was subsequently sent.

'Were you worried about the results?' he asked.

'No,' said Paul.

'No, Father,' prompted Dr Palmer gently and then went on quickly, 'You mean that you didn't care whether you passed or failed?'

'No, Father,' said Paul. He was a handsome boy with fair hair cut short in the schoolboy manner, and slightly slanting grey eyes that gave him a gentle reflective look. Even such obvious questions he answered slowly and deliberately after a moment's hesitation. 'I suppose I felt confident.' His big hands lay openly on the table in front of him and he studied them as he spoke. 'I'm rather interested in Futurism. I enjoyed the examination.'

'Yes. I thought you might have done.' It struck Paul that Dr Palmer might have some advanced knowledge of the results which were not due for another two months. For the first time he looked directly at him. But the psychiatrist's pale drooping face, heavily pouched under the eyes preserved its look of deep melancholy. Paul had disliked him at first, then pitied the irrelevance of his questions. In time, as the interview dragged on, he had come to feel that they were fellow conspirators trying without success to solve the mystery of his wrong-doing.

Dr Palmer began again. 'You see we must both face that what you did was undeniably an act of aggression. There must have been anger in you somewhere, against someone, something. Can you relive for me your feelings just before the fire? Let your mind go back. Try to explain.'

Paul leant back in his chair. He closed his eyes to recapture the darkness and tried again.

'I went for a walk.'

He heard the tiny click of a switch. Previously they had fenced with one another. Now it seemed his words were worth recording.

'Why?'

'I don't know, Father. Suddenly I wanted to go for a walk.'

'But you must have set out with some purpose. To see someone, buy something. People don't just go for walks.'

'I did,' said Paul.

'For how long?' He sounded frankly curious now and this made it easier to talk; besides, these events had happened within the last three days and he felt no fear of losing them.

'I was gone about three hours. I went right across this Estate and the next and the next. I undid my coat. I wanted to feel the cold.' He wondered if he could trust Dr Palmer to understand him. For now that he had begun to talk he wanted to go on, to explain to someone before it was lost to him. 'Right at the top, on the Skeena Hill Estate, there's a place where you can see for miles. I looked south towards the coast, and there for miles and miles were lights. One Estate stretching into another, on and on. There was a kind of glow over everything.'

'What were you thinking about as you looked at it?'

'Over towards Banstead there was one single patch of darkness.'

'Oh yes,' said Dr Palmer, so that Paul broke off.

'What is it?' he asked. 'Why is there nothing there?'

'Oh, but there is. There's a big Recidivist Camp and a Research Centre there. They keep it dark at night.'

In spite of himself Paul shuddered. 'Will I be sent there, Father?'

'Good heavens no,' said Dr Palmer briskly. 'Go on. What were you thinking when you were staring at Banstead?'

'I thought the darkness was like a great black hand. I thought of it as being very strong. I thought that if it wanted to it could move and simply scrape away all those millions of lights, as if they were beads, and leave the entire world black and cold.'

'And then there was the power cut?'

'I didn't know it was that. I thought the hand had moved. I had felt the power. I knew it was there. The cold and the dark. It was tremendous. I began to run.'

'You panicked?'

'In a way, but I knew what to do.'

'At this point did you feel that what you were going to do was wrong?'

Paul thought for a moment. Then he said, slowly and calmly, 'No. It felt right. The only thing to do.'

'So you came back to your own Estate and set fire to the sports pavilion?'

'Yes, Father.'

'And when you had done this, right away did you wish you had not?'

Again Paul considered before he went steadily on, 'I felt tremendously relieved – satisfied that I had done the right thing. I felt that I had saved something precious from a great danger. I almost wished that the lights would stay out so that the flames would be at their most beautiful. When the first people came, I expected them to feel as I did. I was dancing and leaping like the flames. I really thought that they would join me. But they led me away and tried to comfort me. Some of them were weeping at what I had done. Then I came to see that it had all been a terrible mistake. That I had done wrong.'

'But you were convinced as you did it that you were doing right?'

'Oh yes.'

'And then you felt guilt, disgust, repugnance?'

'Not right away,' said Paul.

'When?'

'It was when we got home. Everyone was comforting me. My mother was in a terrible state.'

'You pitied her?'

'It wasn't her so much as our Old Lady.'

'Who is your . . . ?' Dr Palmer glanced quickly down at his notes.

'Great-great-grandmother.'

'Ah,' said Dr Palmer. 'Very old. Pre-Enlightenment. It's marvellous how these old dears cling to life.'

Paul went on. 'When we came back to the flat she'd somehow managed to get out of her chair and crawl to the window and haul herself up. She'd seen the flames.'

'She's senile, isn't she?' said Dr Palmer sharply.

'Yes, perfectly. Normally she is. But she was trying to speak. Normally she doesn't make a sound. She cries sometimes or croons, but these were words.'

'What was she saying?'

'I couldn't understand. But it was horrible. Savage. Like a chant. That made me feel horror at what I had done.

Rum-tum-tum. Rum-tum-tum. Like that. Over and over.'

'Gibberish?'

'No. It meant something. You could tell. It meant something to her. She was saying something about the fire.'

'I'll have to send someone around to see her.' Dr Palmer spoke thoughtfully as if to a colleague. He lifted a pencil, tapped with it for a second on a pad of paper, then wrote.

'You needn't,' said Paul quickly. 'She went straight to sleep. She was quite normal in the morning.'

'No trouble since?'

'None at all.' He wondered what the psychiatrist had written on the paper, but Dr Palmer had laid his large white hand carelessly across it so that Paul could not see. He found himself wishing that all this would end. At the same time he wished the next question would come so that they might move forward again. When there was silence he could not tolerate it for more than a minute, but asked anxiously, 'What will happen to me, Father?'

'Nothing very terrible,' Dr Palmer said, smiling. 'I'll prescribe a tranquilliser for a week or two and put you onto the voluntary welfare scheme. Two hours a day? Could you manage that?'

Paul nodded. 'That's all right. The exams are over.'

'Heard anything yet?'

'Not yet.'

'You may find it rather upsetting – the welfare. It's a client up on the Ackroyden Estate. She's on her own. Three kids.' (*That's illegal for a start*, thought Paul.) 'No husband. There's a pretty useless daughter who's old enough to help, but doesn't. The mother's very ill. She needs odd jobs done. Help with filling in forms. That sort of thing. Maybe she needs help with using the MEMORY.' He had spoken up to now in the fragmented dispassionate voice of a form which was laid neatly beside the folder of notes on Paul's case. Now he glanced up briefly, but seeing Paul's face expressionless, went on. 'She reads a lot. Romances and the like. Harmless enough. We've got some books from the clinic for you to take along. Don't forget all this, will you? Get it all down on your own MEMORY when you get home.'

Paul nodded. Dr Palmer reached under the desk and produced a pile of three books tied together with string. A name, *Mrs E Willmay*, and an address were printed on a slip of paper tucked between the string and the uppermost book. Then he wrote out a prescription and placing it on top of the books, slid the pile across the desk.

Paul stuffed the books into his rucksack and put the prescription carefully into his pocket. The interview was over at last. He stood up.

Dr Palmer leant back in his chair and smiled a sad, kind smile. 'You'll have forgotten all about this in the morning,' he said. 'So will your parents. You can put it right behind you.'

'I know,' said Paul. 'Thank you, Father.'

'Any time,' said Dr Palmer.

CHAPTER TWO

HE WOULD FORGET. He must. But he did not want to.

Outside, the daylight had turned imperceptibly to artificial light. He walked along, shifting the rucksack on his shoulders, trying to imagine again while he could, the sight and sound and smell of the fire. The hand of darkness that had swept over Surrey had been powerful, but the fire he was sure had been more powerful still – and beautiful beyond imagining. To no one but Dr Palmer had he attempted to explain, and then his words had conveyed nothing of his awe, his terror at the thing he had evoked. It was a living thing, or so it had seemed, with breath, force, a voice roaring.

He heard in the street behind him the high-pitched whine of the cleansing machines. The operatives were working late to remove from the caged ornamental trees their dying leaves, before they fell and defaced the pavement outside the Council Offices. He measured it against the sound of fire in his head, but it was a puny thing in comparison. There had been explosions too, loud sharp bangs, which later he had been told were the stored footballs exploding. At the time they had seemed to be shouts of the fire and he had found them particularly satisfying.

His watch told him that it was 5.30.

Behind him, the office blocks towered dark above the brilliantly lit streets. Ahead of him he could see the lighted windows of the flats, stack upon stack of glowing rectangles coloured by their different curtains. He did not hurry. As the psychiatrists worked late so did the chemists. He walked along slowly, blind to the people he passed, playing over and over in his head the sounds of the fire.

As he stood in the queue at the chemist's, holding Dr Palmer's prescription in his hand, he knew that he was slowly losing hold of what had happened to him. Tonight would be the third night. When he woke tomorrow, all trace of it would be gone. He did not want to lose it. He wanted to keep it and think about it until he could understand it better. *I will keep it*, he thought. *It's too powerful to be destroyed.* But he knew in his heart that this was not so, that all he would wake with in the morning was a sense of loss. He thought for a moment of trying to commit it to the MEMORY together with the instructions for his welfare assignment. But it was a wrong-doing. The MEMORY would not record wrong-doings.

When his turn came he took his tube of pills and his receipt from the chemist and walked out into the street holding them and thinking: *I will have lost it all by morning.* He began to walk rapidly towards his own block.

As he approached it he noticed that the Estate operatives had already erected a high fence around the burnt-out pavilion. There was a sign on it saying SPORTS CENTRE IMPROVEMENT SCHEME. Mobile lights had been set at intervals along the perimeter of the fencing. They towered above it, casting a white brilliant light inside. And opened above them were soft purple depths of sky that held a blurred moon and seemed to Paul to be beautiful and strange. From inside the fence he heard the throbbing of a cement mixer. Work would go on all night under the brilliant lights.

He began to hurry again towards home. Minutes later he pushed open the doors of the lobby of his own block. He rose fourteen floors in the lift and let himself into the flat with his own key.

As he took off his weatherproof jacket in the little front hall, he felt the warmth, the beautiful regularity, the changelessness of his home. All returns to it were the same, as if the hands of the clock were set back to the moment of his departure by the turning of his key in the lock. Not that it had stood still waiting for him. Its quiet machinery was always in motion. Now the lamps were lit. He smelt bread baking, warm and delicious; heard his mother singing. She was at the centre of it, working out her steady irreproachable purposes. Even before she appeared, the breath of the home seemed to say, 'This is the only existence. The rest is nothing.'

She was a slight woman coming towards him through the kitchen door, wiping her hands tensely on her apron, staring at him so intently that she seemed to be frowning.

'What happened?' Her whole existence was gathered into the words. He was, of course, her only child. Yet her mind strayed so. A moment ago she had been singing.

'Nothing much,' he said, kissing her. He was taller than she. He held her for a moment by her thin shoulders. He had caused her so much suffering. For two days at the sight of him she had grieved. *But she will forget*, he thought. *Tomorrow she will have forgotten it all*. So that after all he felt a sad acceptance of what tomorrow would do for them.

'What? What will they do to you?'

'Nothing. Welfare work.' He hung the rucksack on the peg beside his jacket.

'What welfare work?'

'A family on the Ackroyden. Too many kids. Sick mother.'

'You won't like the Ackroyden,' said his mother crossly, controlling her joy, her relief that after all no one was going to take him from her. 'It's rough there, not like here.'

'Dad home?' he said.

'Not yet.' She was crying, dabbing at her eyes with the floury hem of her apron.

'Pills for me,' he said, taking the little tube from his pocket.

'Part of the treatment?'

'Yes.'

'Oh go in to your gran,' she said. 'I'm such a fool. I don't know what I thought. Leave me for a minute. Dad'll be home soon. We'll have our Drink.'

He went into the lounge. The old lady sat in her wheelchair by the electric fire, staring into vacancy, plucking with effort at the knitted rug across her knees.

'How's Gran then?' he said, patting the soft weak down through which her old pate shone in patches. 'How's my gran?' He knelt on the hearth rug in front of her.

She smiled then – she always smiled for him – and began to dribble down her chin. He lifted her bib and dabbed gently at the corners of her gathered lips. 'There's a good girl,' he said.

He took her hands in his. 'She's a little cold,' he called out to his mother. There was no answer. He glanced towards the kitchen door. Then, gently, he began to dance the frail old hands up and down on the woollen rug. 'Rum-tum-tum, rum-tum-tum,' he sang softly. Each time, he slackened his own movement to see if any strength came from the old woman's hands, but there was nothing. They lay in his, weightless and lifeless like little bent bundles of dry twigs. Her unfocused eyes groped in the spaces behind him. Her loose smile was an inward thing not relating to him at all.

'She is senile, isn't she?' he called out more loudly to his mother. 'All the time, I mean.'

'Of course,' she called back. When she came to the door of the lounge he could hear the alarm in her voice. 'Why do you ask that?'

'Dr Palmer asked me.'

'There's never been any question,' said his mother. 'I've looked after her since . . . well, she's always been here, hasn't she? She's passed all inspections. She's all right.'

'That's what I said. He believed me.'

Paul waited a minute after his mother had gone back into the kitchen, watching the door. Then he reached into his trouser pocket and took out the box of matches with which he had lit his fire and which, for all their concern for him, no one had thought to take from him. Glancing around once more, he struck one and moved it slowly back and forth in front of the old lady's eyes.

'Rum-tum-tum, rum-tum-tum,' he pleaded with her. The little flame reflected in both pale eyes, but penetrated not at all to the waste beyond. He shook out the match when it was only half spent, and did not expend another.

He put the dead match carefully back into the box and returned it to his pocket. Then he rubbed the old lady's hands for a moment and tucked them gently under the blanket. He turned up the electric fire, kissed her, and went into his own room to record onto his extension of the MEMORY.

Paul's MEMORY stood in its neat plastic casing on a table beside his bed. It was studded with silver buttons and attached to a small paper-shredding machine. He pressed the button marked *Record* and *Play*, typed out his identity number, and began to dictate, first from the carbon copy of the prescription that the chemist had handed him, then the address and the list of instructions from Dr Palmer.

He pushed the button marked *Off*. Before the MEMORY went dead, the message flashed on the screen, NOW DESTROY ALL PAPERS. THIS IS ESSENTIAL TO AVOID CONTAMINATION. Automatically he gathered the papers together for the paper-shredder, but stopped, turning them over in his hand. The other sides were blank. He owned a pencil. It was permitted to use one for calculations in the sixth form. He began to write in close, cramped lines over the backs of the two small sheets; about the power cut, about his fear of the dark, about lighting the fire. He wrote with a kind of desperation: *The flames were an orange colour, not a dead orange like the street lights, but bright . . .* holding the pencil tightly, close to its point, fearing at each second that something would intervene and prevent his doing what he was doing. But he did manage to complete it before he heard his father's key turn in the lock of the front door.

He thought quickly then. He folded, creased and tore off the small blank scrap at the bottom of the second sheet, and fitted onto it the words, *Back of sock drawer*. He fixed the message onto the back of his watch with transparent tape. Then he pulled out one of the top drawers of his chest and neatly taped the other papers to the outside of the back panel, where his mother's care for him would not extend.

He waited in the hall for the mutter of conversation between his parents to subside, then he went into the lounge. His father lay back in his armchair, smiling at him.

Paul's father was an unusually tall man for his times. His size had always frightened Paul, unreasonably, for he had never seen his father angry, let alone felt the weight of his large hand. In spite of his size nothing about him suggested power. If anything, he tried to disguise the girth of those limbs for which he had no use. He kept his hair as short and as sleek as a schoolboy's. He wore his uniform as a senior Estate official a little tight. His rimless spectacles seemed to emphasise the defencelessness of his fresh clear face. He was hard-working, meticulous, a little anxious. He had recently reorganised the filing of relief claims in the extra heating department, and came home at night exhausted. His dearest wish was for Paul to be like him in all things. Tonight, the leniency of Paul's sentence and the knowledge that tomorrow it would all be forgotten left him relaxed and almost happy.

'Thank god it's no worse,' he said.

The curtains were drawn. The room was lit and bright. His mother came in from the kitchen carrying a little tray with three steaming mugs and a drinking bottle.

'That's yours,' she said to Paul, setting his on the mantelshelf.

'I'll do Gran,' he said. He knelt and put his arms around the old lady and fitted the nipple gently between her lips, tilting the bottle carefully so that the liquid stayed at the correct angle. When she had finished he rubbed her back for her. Then he took his own mug from the mantelshelf.

'To you, Paul,' said his father, smiling at him.

The three of them touched their mugs together. 'To the future,' they said. 'To the future. To the future.'

CHAPTER THREE

WHEN PAUL WOKE it was morning. The artificial light was still on, but daylight was overtaking it. He lay gathering in his mind what remained to him of his identity. He was Paul. He was happy. He was loved. His sleepy mind reached out one by one to the people who loved him most, whom most he loved. Mum, Dad, Gran. They were near him. This was his home. The world was a safe place. Home was the safest part of it. He moved his feet under the blanket and stretched his arms out into the warm room. His size was instantly given back to him. He felt hungry and confident that food was near. He smelt a warm smell and could just hear his mother's happy wordless singing. Only at the very remotest corner of his mind did he feel an unaccountable sense of loss. A vanished dream perhaps. For a moment he reached to retrieve it, but it had gone too far.

Nothing lost matters, he told himself. *Nothing is more perfect than this instant. Only the future can exceed it, because the future is an intellectual thing, and therefore truly perfect.* The words did not come to him with the force of thought. They already existed in his mind as if they were a part of its structure.

He reached out and switched on the MEMORY, dialled his identity number and then lay back at his ease while it restored to him what it was necessary for him to know. The MEMORY broadcast that it was Saturday, November 3rd. He felt a surge of pleasure in knowing that all day he could stay among the people whom he most loved. Then his own voice on the MEMORY informed him that this was not so. That in payment of a wrong-doing he must do two hours welfare work on the Ackroyden Estate. The family which he was to visit consisted of three children and a sick mother. He was to take some books which he would find in his rucksack. The MEMORY repeated the address three times slowly so that he might learn it by heart. Then words appeared on the screen. REPEAT INSTRUCTIONS. He typed out on the keyboard the address and the time he was to spend. The words, MESSAGE CORRECTLY INTERPRETED, appeared letter by letter on the screen.

It surprised Paul to learn that he had committed a wrong-doing. He wondered what it might be. He typed, QUERY: WRONG-DOING, and watched the screen with a mild interest. PAUL SIMONDS, it spelt out. WRONG-DOING COMMITTED ON OCTOBER 31st.

He typed, QUERY: NATURE OF WRONG-DOING.

The screen spelt back, CLASSIFIED MATERIAL.

Nothing lost matters.

He switched off then and, following the smell, found his mother setting steaming bowls of cereal on the table onto which cold sun fell brightly now through the uncurtained window.

After lunch he dressed carefully in his outdoor clothes and checked to see that the books were in his rucksack. His mother was giving Gran her bath. He called out to her that he would be gone for three or four hours. He shouldered the rucksack and carefully zipped his outer clothing against the cold.

The air was very clear and bright. He breathed it in, loving the newness of each impression. Hammers rang in the air, sharp and musical as chimes. A new building was going up quite near his home. He walked around the fencing that hid the site from view until he found the sign explaining what it was. He read with interest, SPORTS CENTRE IMPROVEMENT SCHEME. *That's nice*, he thought. *Nice to have one so near.*

He walked across the playing fields that separated his Estate, the Brocklebank, from the Manor Estate. Through the Manor and the underpass that separated it from the Melrose. He crossed the Melrose, went through a second underpass and he was on the Ackroyden. He timed the walk as taking three-quarters of an hour. At intervals he repeated the address, to make sure that he did not lose it.

He found himself at last in a sub-standard area at the very edge of the Estate. Although the grass was clipped immaculately at the front of the building, and the frontage freshly painted, he could see that around the sides, necessary economies had been applied. The sides of the block were unpainted concrete, and the grass at the back that sloped down to the barrier fence of the motorway was rough and wild, nearly a foot high. Set in it was a ramshackle shed, built for some forgotten purpose and never removed. The whole place had an air of neglect and indifference that shocked Paul. *Terrible*, he thought. *Kids, too, growing up in a mess like that.*

He worked out from the table of flat numbers by the lobby entrance that his family would be on the first floor. He felt too nervous to wait for the lift. He ran up the single flight of stairs, and selected the right door on the landing that faced him. He rang the bell and heard it jangle inside. Then footsteps. The door opened and he found himself facing a girl, fifteen or so, sullen, unwelcoming.

'What do you want?' she asked.

'I'm from the welfare,' he said. 'I've some books for Mrs Willmay.'

'Mum,' she called behind her down a dark narrow passage. 'Man from the welfare with some books.' He could hear the hesitation, the hostility from the dark recesses beyond her.

A voice called, 'Bring him in then.'

'Come in then,' she said, making an awkward beckoning motion with her head. He lowered the rucksack from his shoulders, went in past her and headed down the passageway. Dark and wary, the life of this unknown family closed in on him. He thought he heard quick blundering movements in a room ahead of him, an anxious whisper.

'Last on the right,' the girl said behind him.

He paused and opened a door. Three women were sitting around a square table, drinking tea. He noticed that one of them was very fat and that one of them presented to him her back and a mat of ageless blonde hair. Between sips of tea they were smoking cigarettes, and a saucer set between them on the table was heaped with ash and stubbed ends. The artificial light was on. A thin red cotton curtain was drawn across the window through which the sinking sun burnt in a single intense spot of light.

He saw at once that they had been enjoying themselves and that he had intruded upon their pleasure, and somehow spoilt it. It made him feel unsure, unhappy. *What am I supposed to do here?* he wondered. The rucksack strap dragged at his hand. He thought of the books.

'Mrs Willmay?' he asked.

'That's me.' It was the fat woman who answered. Swollen arms protruded from the short sleeves of her dress.

Her hands, cradling the mug of tea, were thick and square and coarse like a man's, but creased at the wrist like a baby's. Her features were obscured by the bunched masses of her cheeks and chin. Even her eyes were magnified and partially concealed by the thick lenses of her spectacles.

'I'm Paul Simonds,' he said. 'I'm from the welfare.'

He could tell that for some reason she was suspicious, even afraid of him, that when she said in a deep pleasant voice, 'Well, sit down then, Paul. Have a cup of tea,' she was merely sounding friendly. All the time the other women were summing him up. The girl lingered behind him somewhere, half in, half out of the room.

Cautiously he took his place on the bench on which the blonde woman was sitting. She nodded to him and shifted a little away from him.

'My mate, Jeanie,' said Mrs Willmay, by way of introduction.

'How do you do,' said Paul.

'Very well, thank you,' said Jeanie, smiling stiffly at him out of an old face oddly framed in the young yellow hair.

'This is Rose,' said Mrs Willmay. The third woman had an old face too, but the soft puckered skin was so carefully painted over with a young blooming face that Paul felt he was watching two faces at once, one smooth and pretty and guileless, the other shrewd. 'She's my home help,' said Mrs Willmay. They exchanged bows. 'The other two kids are out playing. Do you want to see them?'

'No,' said Paul. 'I just brought some books.'

'Well, Sharon, fill up the pot,' said Mrs Willmay, trying, it seemed, to lighten the atmosphere by an effort of voice.

The girl took the pot from the table, and filled it at the stove, and returned it. The sound of its tin lid shutting and its contact with the table entered Paul's ears like abuse.

'I've brought you some books,' he said again to Mrs Willmay. He bent down and took them from his rucksack.

'Oh yes,' said Mrs Wilmay. He noticed that she did not even glance at them as he handed them to her. He wondered if, having delivered them, he might go. He tried to tell himself that the hour and a half walk there and back counted towards the two hours of his amendment.

'Is there anything else I could do for you while I'm here?'

'No,' she said. 'No, not that I can think of.'

He said lamely, 'I'm meant to stay two hours. It's an amendment.'

'Oh gawd,' she said. 'I've nothing will take two hours. Not with a home help and Sharon – not that she's much help.'

'No,' said Jeanie, pitching her voice towards the door where the girl had taken up position again on the very frontier of the room. 'She's a bad girl and doesn't help her mother as she should. Not as things are.'

The girl did not answer nor so much as look at her. She stood with her back to the edge of the open door, her hands behind her each holding a knob. She began to swing it and herself, so that with each motion it creaked.

Suddenly the mother was shouting, bunched cheeks shaking with rage, 'Oh for gawdsake, give over doing that, Sharon, won't you!' Then she pressed the swollen dimpled hands to her head and shook it this way and that.

The suddenness and unfamiliarity of such an outburst made Paul start uncontrollably.

Mrs Willmay did not apologise for shouting, but spoke so gently then to Paul that it seemed like an apology. 'Did they tell you at the welfare that I was ill? I don't exactly look as if I were fading away, do I?'

She was coaxing him, urging him to think well of her, to forget that she had shouted, to forgive her for being fat. He would have liked to help her. He said, 'Yes. As a matter of fact they did.'

'What did they say?' she asked eagerly. 'They don't tell me much.'

'Just that. That you were ill.'

'They're just keeping me going on the drugs,' said Mrs Willmay. 'They say there's no hope for me otherwise.' The voice was unutterably bleak.

The room had fallen very silent. The two other women sat still, staring down at the table top. The girl stood leaning against the motionless door, her eyes fixed on the cold red sunspot in the curtain. He could see no trace of emotion on her face.

From behind the curtain there came quite clearly into the strained silence, a little ringing rattle. The sound seemed to rouse Mrs Willmay. 'But I'm tougher than they think,' she said. 'I've a few surprises left for them.' Her voice warmed, thickened with laughter, drew them towards her again. *Don't go away*, she was saying, *don't go away because I am ill.*

Rose, the help with the precarious red curls, got up from the bench and knelt beside Mrs Willmay's chair. 'That you have, my darling,' she declared fiercely, stroking the fat hand. 'They don't know what they're up against in you.'

'You'll show them, Ellie,' said Jeanie.

'Give us a refill then,' said Mrs Willmay, quite restored. She held forward a shaky cup, and when Paul shyly filled it, she said, with formal friendliness, 'Only you in the family then?'

He nodded. 'And my gran.'

'Oh,' she said indulgently. 'Oh, you've an Old Lady. Oh it's nice to have an Old Lady in the family. Jeanie has her gran, haven't you, Jeanie?'

'Had her always,' said Jeanie. 'She's a dear old thing really, no trouble at all, is she, Ellie?'

'No, she's lovely. I love your gran. You should see her someday if you've time,' she said to Paul, 'really you should. She's got ever such pretty hair, hasn't she, Jeanie?'

'I did it up with a bow this morning. She looked a treat.'

'You should have brought her in to see me. She's lovely

hair,' Mrs Willmay said again to Paul. 'Your gran very old then?'

He shrugged and smiled at her. 'Oh very old. Mum says she was old ever so long ago when she took her over.'

'It's lovely if you can have them with you,' she said. Then the sadness returned to her voice. 'I've a gran somewhere. They won't let me have her with me. They took her away.'

He knew at once that she had said something she ought not to have said. He saw the two women look quickly, tensely, at one another, then at him. At the same time, like a talisman against evil, the words filled his mind: *Nothing lost matters*. But what was it that she had said? He could not think.

Mrs Willmay lay back in her chair with her eyes shut. Moisture shone on the pouched skin below them. Perhaps she was crying. The room was very quiet again. From behind the curtain he heard the same odd scratching sound, but his mind was taken up with Mrs Willmay.

She said, 'I loved my gran. She was very old. Pre-Enlightenment, they said. They took her away years ago. She must be dead by now.'

Nothing lost matters, clamoured his brain, but at the same moment he realised with shock and discomfort that he was hearing someone speak about the past time.

'Didn't I say it wasn't working,' said Jeanie to Rose. 'They'll have her out of here in no time flat, if they get to hear of this,' and she directed towards Paul a look of such

32

bitter suspicion that he feared her.

'I'd never tell,' he said. He felt nothing but pity for her, and a gnawing fear for himself of contamination. He did not know what he should do.

'They'd never let her stay in a house where there's kiddies, talking like that,' said Jeanie.

Sharon broke out into loud harsh sobs and ran from the room.

'Give over,' shrieked Jeanie after her. 'Give over, will you, and get her her Drink. It can't hurt her to give it her a little early.'

'She had it early last night, so we gave her a bit at noon,' said Sharon in her loud abusive voice.

'So what are we to do?' whispered Rose. 'We've got to stop her.'

Mrs Willmay ignored them all. 'I wish she were here,' she said. 'I often think of her coming in that door. "What ever's happened to you, Ellie?" she'd say. "What'd you let yourself get fat for?"' She laughed. '"And look at Sharon all grown up, and the little ones."'

'Stop her, for gawdsake, can't you? Stop her, Sharon, can't you?'

'"Look at this dump then," she'd say. "What you living in a place like this for then, Ellie? You and your grand ideas. What ever's happened to you?"'

'Nothing lost matters, Mum,' said Sharon in a shocked and gentled voice.

'That's right,' said Jeanie, looking gratefully at the girl. 'Nothing lost matters.'

'That's right, Ellie,' urged Rose. 'Nothing lost matters.'

But Mrs Willmay ignored them all. 'I wish she'd come. When it starts to get cold and dark at night, I think of her, just lately. I think of her wandering about the streets in the dark and the cold, with nowhere to go.'

She was only stopped by the sudden loud ringing of the doorbell. Sharon slid out of the room. They heard her walk without haste down the passage. They all sat listening, together, Paul, drawn in with them, feeling with them curiosity mingled with the fear of intrusion.

They heard the girl open the front door and say crossly, 'What ever do you lot want?'

But cutting across her last words came the thin jeering voices of children. They sat quite silent around the table listening to the chant of indistinguishable words. The cold air penetrated from outside, but no one moved to close the kitchen door. The small slurred voices reached them as from another planet.

'Well that's a new one,' said Jeanie. 'Little devils. What do you suppose they're after?'

'What is it?' whispered Rose. 'What is it?'

'Gives me the creeps,' muttered Jeanie.

Only Mrs Willmay seemed unperturbed. 'They've come for the cakes,' she said. 'I've only biscuits, but I've not been well. I'm sure they'll not mind.'

The others stared at her. Like someone in a trance, she braced her great arms on the table and slowly heaved herself to her feet. She reached down a square biscuit tin from the shelf and began to shuffle with it out of the door and down the corridor.

'She's worse,' whispered Rose when she had gone. 'You see it, coming every day as I do. She's gone way down just lately.'

Jeanie tightened her eyes shrewdly. 'If you ask me, I'd say the drugs weren't working as they did.'

'Well, this is it,' said Rose. 'Too many, and they start to cancel each other out.'

'Here,' Jeanie said to Paul. 'You go and see that she's all right. That Sharon's worse than useless.'

Mrs Willmay had not reached the front door. She had stopped halfway down the passage and leant her back against the wall, panting slightly and struggling to loosen the lid of the biscuit tin. Sharon stood watching her, making no move to help. The eerie voices had begun again. Now he was near enough to try to make out the words.

'So, so, for a so kay,' they chanted. It meant nothing to him.

The tin lid came away as he reached Mrs Willmay. 'Help me,' she whispered. 'They've come for the cakes. But biscuits will have to do.' He took her arm and she leant heavily on it the few steps to the door.

'Give them the biscuits,' she said to Sharon. But at the

sight of her, the children, dirty wretched-looking little things, suddenly fled as if in terror.

It was that strange hour when the weak evening light seemed to struggle for mastery with the artificial, knowing that it could not win. The naked bulb shone feebly in the stale passageway. He could hear the irregular beat of the children's flight down the concrete staircase. Their bird voices rose in thin shrieks up the lift shaft.

'*One for Peter, one for Paul.*'

'That's you, isn't it?' said Mrs Willmay. 'Your name is Paul.'

'Yes,' he said.

She was shaking with cold before Sharon finally closed the door. He began to lead her back to the warm kitchen. Now the other women emerged and helped her back to her chair.

'She's stone cold,' said Jeanie reproachfully, glaring at Sharon. 'You'd no business leaving the door open like that. Little devils. What did they want anyway?'

'Poor soul,' said Rose, staring down at Mrs Willmay in her chair. 'She looks done in. Poor soul.'

But Mrs Willmay lifted her head then and stared at Rose acutely. 'Soul,' she repeated. 'Soul cakes. That's what they'd come for. Soul cakes. Poor souls. Poor hungry souls.'

'They were never hungry, little bleeders. I'll have something to say to them if they come back.'

Soul, thought Paul. '*Poor soul*' *meant* '*Poor sick person*'. *But soul cake? What then was soul?*

Mrs Willmay began to sing in a voice surprisingly rich and full, '*Soul, soul for a soul cake.*' But then, like one of his mother's wordless songs, it broke off and was gone.

There was a long silence.

'I've nothing for you to do,' said Mrs Willmay, smiling at him. 'Come back another day and I'll think of something.'

Sharon was sent with him to the door.

'Goodbye,' he said. But she didn't answer. As he ran down the stairs he thought he heard another footstep following, but he knew better than to look back. Outside, he walked as fast as he could without running over the rough grass. Behind him, a voice, taunting and malicious, chanted, '*One for Peter, one for Paul.*' Two stones flew past him. He didn't turn around. He didn't know whether they had been thrown by the sullen girl or by the goblin children.

He walked rapidly downhill through the dusk. All the way he passed Estate officials and operatives trooping home under the yellow lights, dark stooped shapes, their uniforms merged one against another, indistinguishable, with the lamp light reflecting on bald heads and white heads and dark heads. Once or twice above the shuffling of boots and the endless sibilance of the motorways, he thought he heard the clatter of frightened feet and the cold lilt of singing voices, but he could not be sure. He looked up at the sky, but could see nothing, no moon, no stars, for the haze of orange light reflected on low cloud. He began to hurry as he came closer to home. As he emerged from the underpass leading to his own Estate he felt immense relief.

All the details of it, distinct and colourless in the artificial light, seemed superior to the places he had left. The neatly trimmed grass, the symmetrically clipped caged trees, the swept paths, all promised order and certainty. Never had he felt such love for it. He felt it to be the best, most significant place in the world. The chance that he might not have belonged to it seemed too horrible to contemplate. When he passed the new sports pavilion where the operatives still worked under arc lights, he felt a wave of pride that he should be part of it.

His mother hurried into the hall as he unlocked the door.

'You're late,' she said. 'Are you all right?'

'Yes.' He laughed as he kissed her. 'Yes. perfectly all right.'

'I don't like you going there. It's a rough place.'

'It's nicer here.'

'I should hope so,' she said indignantly. 'Come.' She pulled him by the hand into the lounge, and he knew that she had something to show him, something she had made or done during the day to show her love, her pride in her family. He was afraid that he would fail to notice, but to his relief it was unmistakable. Spread over his grandmother's knees was a new rug, crocheted in tiny patches of bright yarn. It seemed the more miraculous to him that it should be so large and intricate, for he had no clear image of seeing his mother work on it. She, too, stared at it in proud wonder, fingering the corner of it. He knew to take his time praising it, the colours and the pattern. 'I'll just put it on her tonight,' she said, 'to show you and your father. Then I'll fold it away until we wheel her out.'

'She'll be the smartest of the lot, won't you, Gran?' He knelt in front of the wheelchair holding the old lady's hands, and as he knelt the little boys' chant sang unsummoned in his head. It seemed a cold, wild, disreputable thing brought in out of the night, having no place here.

'Oh wash your hands,' said his mother. 'I don't like you touching her when you've been in that place.'

He, too, wanted to wash, wanted to wash the confused words out of his mind.

He went into his room and filled the basin so deep with hot water that he thought to remove his watch and lay it on the little shelf below the mirror. He scrubbed his hands carefully with soap and a brush. Then before he left the room he went over to the MEMORY.

He dialled his identity number. Then he typed out, QUERY: THE MEANING OF SOUL, and watched the answering letters appear one by one on the screen.

THE PORTION OF THE MIND THAT ASPIRES TO THE FUTURE.

The MEMORY repeated the message three times and Paul repeated the words, mouthing them, possessing them. 'The soul is that portion of the mind that aspires to the future.'

What then was a soul cake?

He knew better than to ask.

CHAPTER FOUR

'HOW'S THE WELFARE work, boy?' said Paul's father from his chair. The Drink had been shared, the future toasted, supper was eaten and cleared. Paul, standing by the window, had drawn back the curtains by the length of an arm, and with his forehead resting on the cold pane stared into the brightly lit night. He felt tighten inside him the hard knot of anxiety that his father's questions always produced. They had been alone in the room for some minutes while his mother settled Gran for the night. So heavy was the silence between them that they could hear her crooning song and the rhythmic squeak of the bed's wheels as she pushed it gently to and fro.

His father's question came like an insistence that he should turn his attention back into the room. Very slowly Paul turned and leant against the window ledge, facing him.

'Not bad, really.'

'I've never liked it up the Ackroyden. They're a rough lot up there.' When Paul said nothing, he added, 'What are they like?'

'Not bad,' said Paul slowly. 'Not vicious or anything. Quite nice really.' The fat woman who had shouted and spoken of the past, had no place in this room. It was too difficult to discuss her except in terms that would be acceptable and reassuring.

'What did you do?'

'Nothing much. Just had tea with her. I took her some books. She said she'd give me something to do tomorrow.'

'What's the flat like?'

'Not bad, really,' said Paul. 'The girl's rather awful. Still.' He turned to stare out of the window again. It cost him an effort to keep his legs still, to stop his hand from plucking at the curtain. All the time a wild restlessness made him long to be outside. He stared down at the streets pricked out below him in bright yellow lights, each set in a tight thicket of paler rays. The lighted blocks of flats stretched away as far as he could see. In the nearby blocks, irregular patches of windows were distinct. In the distance they were merely built of layers of dark and light rising thickly into the night sky.

'I think I'll go out,' said Paul.

'What for?' said his father. 'It's dark.'

'It's not really dark,' said Paul. 'You can see just as well.'

'You know your mother wouldn't like it.'

He shrugged. 'There's no substandard housing on this Estate, is there?'

'There's a little,' said his father. 'There's not much need for it here, but there's a little. All Estates are built with a little.'

'I've never seen it.' It disturbed him to think that his Estate should be marred by such a place.

'You've not missed much. And don't you go hanging about there now,' for Paul was making towards the door. 'They can be really rough, those gangs of boys off the substandards.'

'I just want to see what they're like.'

'They're all just the same.'

'Shan't be long.' His heart was beating. He really feared his father might prevent his going. He knew he must be gone before his mother reappeared.

He zipped up his jacket in the lift and went out into the street, hunching his shoulders against the cold, and sinking his chin into its collar, so that his warm breath stayed around his face. At first he just walked, staring at his own feet as they moved in and out of his circle of vision on the brightly lit pavement. Then when his steps took on a rhythm and the distance from home lengthened, he lifted up his head and turned it from side to side as he walked, absorbing everything he could see or smell.

He walked straight ahead, knowing that in time he

must reach the periphery of the Estate. He guessed that the substandard housing would be situated somewhere along it, as it had been on the Ackroyden. He would circle around the edge until he found it. He did not want to believe that conditions like that existed on his Estate. He would have to see it really to believe.

The streets were quiet now; the workers all returned to flats like his own, sitting in chairs as his father did, or lying already on their beds, staring at the ceiling, waiting for sleep to come. He felt the weight of all their stationary lives stacked layer on lighted layer on either side of him all the length of the straight street.

But the streets themselves, although they seemed empty, were alive. He could feel running through them the currents of restlessness that animated him, jerked his legs along, made him swing his arms elaborately as he walked. Passing the mouths of side streets, he heard the sudden rattle of footsteps as if boys watched and veered away at his approach. Here and there small groups of boys leant against walls under the street lights, watching him pass. They did not call out, nor did he look too closely at any of them, feeling a danger and excitement he did not want to challenge even with his eyes. He feared them. He liked fearing them. He knew that the same restlessness that had dragged him out had worked on them. They were about the same unknown business, but separate as he was separate.

The murmur of the sunken motorway was louder now,

and soon he could see ahead the unlighted area of ground marking its route between the lighted

He found a boundary road and began to follow it. It seemed he smelt burning – a sweet pungent smell. Now and then between the blocks of dwellings he saw glowing smudges that might have been fires smouldering in the wide embankment leading down to the motorway. He told himself that they were empty tins or fragments of glass that had caught the light. Still, he breathed in deeply to catch that elusive smell of burning. More than ever the outside night seemed alive.

When he came to the substandard area he found it considerably smaller than on the Ackroyden, but otherwise identical: the poor lighting, the painting confined to the facade of the blocks, the rough unmown grass at the rear. He went down the lane by the first block to get behind the houses. It was darker than he was accustomed to; the backs of these flats were unlit on the outside, but never entirely dark. Diagonal shafts of light streamed from uncurtained windows in the flats above, describing sharply lit patches in the long grass. He heard the hum of the motorway like a single ceaseless engine, but closer, clearer, the sound of running footsteps beat out on the hard ground like an excited heart.

There was scuffling, whispering, as if there were children all about him, but hiding from him. Before his eyes had grown used to the poor light, he heard a burst of stifled laughter away to his left. He waited, blinking his eyes to help them see. Above, a shaft of light vanished into blackness, darkening the grass, and a moment later another flashed down like a spotlight a few yards away, catching in its bright rectangle a close troop of children. He heard them squeal and scatter. Something bumped wildly after them across the rough grass, a little box on wheels in which lay slumped the body of a smaller child in a red coat. The little head in its red hood lurched as the cart lurched, making no attempt to steady or protect itself. He felt the sudden terrible conviction that it was injured, even dead. That they intended it nothing but evil.

He began to run after them, horrified at what he might find, but compelled to find it. In a moment he was in amongst them, far bigger than they, grabbing at a coat, then an arm. The small boy he captured was thin, but surprisingly strong. He twisted ferociously to get free. The others vanished without a sound other than their frightened panting.

With one hand he gripped cruelly to the boy's bony wrist. With the other he groped about in the dark for the wagon. 'What's in it?' he hissed. 'What's in it?'

'Nothing,' said the boy sullenly.

'There's something in it. I saw it.'

His fingers closed around the rope by which the cart had been hauled and he tugged it back into the patch of light, dragging the boy with him.

Immediately his hand was on the rope his panic subsided, for he could feel that whatever it was was inhumanly weightless. When he had dragged it back into the patch of light, he looked down and saw a dolly dressed in child's clothes, like those the old ladies liked to rock and press against themselves. He looked at it in disgust. He knew it was nothing, but still it frightened him. It stared up with a white featureless circle of cloth for a face. Out of the cuffs of the coat and leggings poked tufts of grass, tied with string.

'What is it?' he said to the little boy. He was almost whispering now. It was an unnatural thing.

'It's not for anything,' said the boy. 'Let me go.' He was very young. Five. Maybe less, with a pale untrusting wedge of a face; frightened of Paul, but acting the part of some older child who isn't frightened.

'Did you make it?'

'Me and my mates, yeah. What's it to you?'

'You don't play with dollies!'

'No,' he said, off his guard with indignation. 'It's not a dolly.'

'What is it then?'

The boy looked down at his feet and muttered, 'A guy,' so indistinctly that Paul said, 'What?' The word was quite unfamiliar to him. 'What is it?'

'A guy.'

'What's that?'

The child looked him desperately in the eye then and blurted out like an incantation that would free him, *'Remember, remember the fifth of November.'*

'Say it again,' said Paul. 'Say it again slowly and I'll let you go.'

The child repeated sullenly and without conviction, for it had failed him in his need, 'Remember, remember –'

'What?' said Paul. 'What's that word?'

'Re-mem-ber.'

'Remember? What does it mean?'

'How'd I know?' said the child. His voice was breaking now. He tugged wretchedly at his wrist, forcing Paul to hurt him or free him. 'It's all rubbish. It doesn't mean a thing. It's what you're meant to say when you've a guy. It's rubbish.'

'Say it again, slowly.'

'Re-mem-ber.'

'Where did you learn it. Where did you learn those words?'

'I don't know,' said the boy, who had begun to cry. 'They were in my head. No one put them there. None of the older boys knew it. They made me say it. I'm sick of saying it.'

Paul let him free. The child was gone at once, the cart bumping after him.

Paul walked back towards home saying to himself, 'Remember, remember.' He would lose it at any moment. He would lose it. It went in sound with November.

Remember, November. He turned off the road and stood for a few minutes on one of the motorway bridges where the traffic roar drowned all other sounds. He called down softly to the chasing cars below. 'Remember, remember, remember.'

He let himself into the flat, went straight to his own room, and changed into his pyjamas. He washed first his hands and then his face, felt for a towel, rubbed at his face, rubbed at the clouded glass, then stared, blinking, at his reflection, feeling a sense of displacement he could not explain. It amounted almost to fear. He wanted to be back in the lounge with his parents and to be assured of their recognition and acceptance. He saw that he had left his watch on the shelf under the mirror. He picked it up by its face and felt something unmetallic on the back. Turning it over, he read, *Back of sock drawer*. It was quite meaningless, yet confronted with his own handwriting, he knew that he had written something and unaccountably hidden it. It was important, but it was wrong. Already, before it was time, his mind strained to reject it. At the same time the questions were insistent and painful. What had he written? Why should he hide it? He stood staring stupidly at his message for several seconds, then drew out the drawer in which socks were neatly rolled in balls and fitted in tight ranks. He felt carefully at the back. He pulled the drawer out further so that it nearly fell. Then he lifted it out altogether and took out a handful of socks to make sure that whatever it was had not slipped under them. It was as he replaced them that he noticed the papers stuck to the outside of the back panel, reflected in the mirror. He carefully stripped off the tape that held them and hiding them in his pocket, replaced the drawer. He sat on the bed and switched on his bedside lamp and unfolded the paper. On one side of the first sheet was Mrs Willmay's address in a hand he did not know. On the other side, close, tight writing, line after line – his own writing again. He began to read his own forgotten voice.

I watched the dark area. I thought, what holds it in? What if it spreads? At that moment there seemed to be an explosion of darkness, as if the dark were a source of energy so powerful that nothing could control it. I knew I must do something to stop the dark spreading. The lights came on again, but the dark had been sufficiently powerful to wipe them out. It was necessary to do something. When I passed the sports pavilion I knew what I must do. There were cans of petrol in the storeroom for the team van, and boxes of matches. I emptied petrol on the floor and tossed it at the curtains. I struck a match and threw it onto the pool of petrol and ran outside. At first I hid. I watched the smoke work out from under the door and the windows. Then there was a little glow. I could see it through the window. I felt very happy. I had done the necessary thing, and now I knew that everything would be all right. If only the fire went well. If it grew stronger. Through the window I could see the flames running up the curtain. I willed it to be stronger, to break out of the prison of the pavilion. The smoke was coming out all around the door, like mist, and out between the tiles on the roof. Then there was a little line of flame on the roof. The flames were an orange colour, not a dead orange like the street lights, but bright. I came out of hiding then because I knew everything was all right. I knew the light had won. It was strong enough. I began to shout. I began to jump with the flames. I was strong. I made the flames strong. I was very happy. I saw the people coming. I thought they were coming to dance with me.

There it stopped. The end of the second sheet seemed to have been torn off.

It was utterly inconceivable that he should do anything so wrong, so senselessly destructive. He had no recollection of the fire, but he realised that what he had read must have happened. He was making amends for some wrongdoing. They were rebuilding the pavilion. It was possible. In his own writing he had written that he had done this, and at the moment of doing so had believed it right. He must believe that too. He thought of his mother and immediately felt overcome with gratitude and relief that no trace of this remained in her mind. The thought of her finding it, reading it, being forced to suffer again as she must briefly have suffered was so appalling to him that he took the papers in both hands, one one way and one the other, to tear them from top to bottom and feed the bits to the paper-shredder. But he found he could not do it. What he had written was too precious to him. He read it again, thought for a moment and then reaching out slowly to the MEMORY, dialled his identity number. He typed out, QUERY: NATURE OF MY RECENT WRONG-DOING.

The answer flickered across the screen, CLASSIFIED INFORMATION.

He read the paper again. He had found a way to steal from the MEMORY.

He realised then that the MEMORY must steal from him.

Nothing lost matters, clamoured his mind. He read the paper again. He thought this must matter and yet it had been taken entirely out of his mind. *With how much else*, he thought. He felt the same sensation of rising panic of which he had written when he described the area of darkness over Banstead. He felt the normality that surrounded and contained him suddenly powerless against it.

The memory was his enemy. He had found a way to outwit it. He folded the papers and slid them into his pyjama pocket again. He would keep them with him always. Then he reached his finger cautiously towards the MEMORY and typed out, QUERY: THE MEANING OF REMEMBER.

The pause that followed seemed endless. *Is it broken*, he thought. Then, letter by letter, the answer built itself. THIS MORPHEME/GRAPHEME COMBINATION EMBODIES NO KNOWN CONCEPT.

But he was sure that the child had said it so, and his conviction was made the fiercer by knowing that on the following morning he would be less sure and that on the morning following that he would have lost the word for ever. He pressed the query button and began to spell out the word again, sounding it carefully as he spelt, stabbing out the letters on the keys as if to convey his anger into the mind of the MEMORY.

R-E-M-E-M-B-E-R

The screen stayed blank. Then the bright letters flicked onto it one after the next.

THIS MORPHEME/GRAPHEME COMBINATION EMBODIES NO . . .

He switched it off in disgust.

The closing message flashed on the screen: NOW DESTROY ALL PAPERS. THIS IS ESSENTIAL TO AVOID CONTAMINATION.

Paul felt for his pencil, unfolded the paper and wrote defiantly on the narrow margin: *Remember, remember, remember.*

CHAPTER FIVE

THE FOLLOWING DAY was Sunday when life hung in suspension and families kept together within the confines of their homes.

On the Monday afternoon, after his last lesson at school, Paul turned away from home and set out again for the Ackroyden and Mrs Willmay. He went because he had no choice but to go. It was an amendment, but at the same time it almost seemed to be excitement that hurried him up the hill, looking this way and that for the phantom troop of children that had sung their strange song that first afternoon.

He was walking alone, but in a procession of boys released from schools like his; some like himself with heads sometimes bowed, sometimes thrown back to relish the cold air and watch the cold, sick sun fail against the close battlements of the tower blocks.

As it fell it transformed long columns of windows into flaming burnished metal. But they too, he supposed, would be cold if you could reach out your hand to them, false fires lit by a failing sun.

Other boys walked along in groups of four or six together, swaying into each other, bumping, stumbling, barring the road, then breaking into ragged clusters, jumping, twisting, animated by some aimless force that had crouched inside them through the long hours of lessons waiting for the crack of light at the door, the moment of release.

He walked through the Ackroyden to the substandard housing on the far side. Lights were beginning to show in the windows. At the entrance to the block he saw the girl, Sharon, standing by the open lobby door, and a row of children's heads black against the light inside. He stopped and watched them, aware that his heart was beating rapidly. Then he realised that they were going in under the arch of Sharon's arm. They must be Mrs Willmay's younger children and the friends with whom they had played.

'Well,' she called out to him. 'Are you coming or aren't you?' Little enough, but something in her tone made him feel that she had relented towards him. As he approached she stood watching, not him but the sky, hungrily as if her few minutes duty opening and shutting the door were all she ever saw of it.

'Not a very nice day,' she said, still looking up at the sky.

He dared to smile at her, but she never met his eyes.

She slammed the door behind him and ran up the steps beside the lift shaft, shouting ahead of him to the smaller children, 'Take your boots off before you go inside.'

A boy's voice protested loudly from the door of the flat, 'We're going right out again.'

'What do I care if you're going out again. Take your boots off in the house.'

When Paul reached the landing, the door was open. A boy, no more than five, had dropped onto the floor of the hall. He was dragging off his boots and hurling them at the wall. Paul smiled at him too, but he only stared in return through dark round eyes, overhung with a fringe of brown hair, and ran before him into the kitchen.

Sharon, leant against the kitchen door, said, 'Peter!'

Paul stepped over the boots and went past her into the kitchen. Mrs Willmay sat in her chair dispensing biscuits. Children clustered around her, clamouring, and the little girl was thrusting at her a heavily painted cardboard construction of some sort, a faded triumph from the distant morning, so that in a moment Mrs Willmay's joy at seeing them had died and she said crossly, 'That's enough. That's enough.'

'Can we go out?' said the boy.

'Yes, but put your boots on.'

'Sharon made me take them off.'

'Well, put them on again.' Her little hoard of energy

had been expended in a minute. She leant her heavy face against the back of the chair, quite drained of colour, her whole exhausted bulk crying fatigue.

'How do you feel?' asked Paul, sitting on one of the benches.

'Rotten,' she said. 'It's bad temper keeps me going.'

'Can I make you a cup of something?' he asked shyly, fearing that she might think he was asking for himself.

'Oh, would you?' she said. 'Just pop the kettle on. Sharon will make it. Sharon?' she called. No answer. 'She's gone out to play,' said Mrs Willmay. 'There'll be tears. You'll see. They play quite happily for hours, then she joins them and there's trouble. She's too big for play anyway. She ought to be in here making tea.'

'It's hard on her,' said Paul. 'Knowing you're ill.'

'You don't see her shedding any tears. She's hard as nails. She doesn't do a thing for me.'

He leant against the stove, not knowing what to say. At a little rattling sound, his eyes strayed to the window. Then he noticed that today the curtain was not drawn and that in the window recess was a living creature in a cage. The name came slowly from a school book. A bird. It should not, of course, have been there. Animals, birds, plants are incompatible with any sort of standard of living worthy of the Estates. There is always the fear of contamination. He supposed that was why they had hidden it before. There had been the small sounds and the tension on his arrival.

Now Mrs Willmay said, 'We thought we could trust you not to tell.'

'Yes. Of course.' The pleasure of being included quite wiped away any scruple he might have had about their keeping the bird, any fear for himself of contamination. 'Aren't you afraid of inspection?'

'They don't inspect the substandards. Not properly. They think us hopeless,' she said with a grunting laugh.

'Where did you get it?'

He went over to the cage to stare at it curiously. It was a sickly little bird with green and red feathers, hunched on its perch. He felt distaste for it. 'It doesn't look very well.'

'No,' she said, 'I expect it will go before I do. It pines in the cage, but I daren't let it free. There's nothing for it to live on. It's not strong enough.' Her voice was full of sorrow, and he felt suddenly sad for the sick woman, the sickly bird, the failing sun.

'I expect if I go first, Sharon will let it go. She's never been bothered about it, so best it dies.'

He poured the tea into a mug and brought it to her, hoping to distract her. 'Oh that tastes good,' she said to him. 'Oh that's what I needed.' She asked him about school, and as they sipped companionably at the hot tea he told her about the course on Futurism he would study next autumn in the university section. How he hoped to become a planner.

'You'll be posh then,' she said, looking at him almost

coquettishly over her spectacles. 'Too posh to come visiting me.'

'No,' he said, blushing. 'No, of course not.'

When he had washed up the mugs he asked, 'Is there anything I can do?'

She asked him to help her with her MEMORY. It was an old model, less sophisticated than his, but he worked out in a minute how to use it. She said it confused her, and he noticed how dusty it was. It seemed a thing she had little interest in. Still, with his help she compiled lists of food to order tomorrow, of clothes to ask of the Welfare for the children, the meter readings, the endless prescriptions. Occasionally as she dictated, shouts from the space behind the block could be heard, sharpened by the cold air outside.

'Are they all right?' he asked her once. It was quite dark outside now.

'Yes,' she said, and added quite at variance to what she had said before, 'Sharon's with them.'

When the recording was finished she sighed and seemed to brace herself in her chair. 'Go and call them, would you?'

He let himself out of the flat and ran down the stairs by the lift. At the back of the lobby he found another door. He went out into the partially lit mysterious landscape he had visited on his own Estate two nights before. But the shafts of light that had fallen from the backs of those houses were not there. Looking up, he saw that every window was curtained and blinded, refusing to see or to be seen to be seeing. For unmistakably a fire had been lit in the grass. He could smell it, strong and exciting, but between him and it there was an irregular black fence of children's heads and merging bodies. The flames leapt above their heads and then sank. As he came down the embankment the fence of children parted.

He could see the fallen fire, black and red, spread over the blackened grass, and then, with the same sense of ancient alarm that had entered him at the sight of the baby figure being dragged in the cart, he saw two taller figures struggling. A boy dragging a girl – Sharon, by her height and lank hair. Closer and closer to the fire. And she dragging back at arm's length, her head turned back, while the little children cheered and laughed and she, he thought, screamed, though that, too, might have been laughter.

He was running to drag her from the flames, when suddenly he experienced a violent lift of comprehension, a certainty of what was right and necessary. This was what had happened before, what he had written on the paper.

He did not run, he leapt, tossing up his arms like flames, his legs danced like flames. His body twisted like flames. They saw him coming and cheered, and the cheering made him more of a flame until he had Sharon by the other hand, dragging her towards the embers, tossing up her arm with his, smelling the sharp frightened sweat on her dress, lifting her with his leap, with his arms, with his great loud voice, all the unwanted strength accumulated in him, released, exploded over the dying flames to urge them up again; then down into the embers burning through the soles of his shoes. And again with the other boy on the other side, but he leapt higher this time, pouring more strength, leaping more light and she with him, her face turned towards him so that they breathed in each other's laughter out of the smoke-filled air. Again. Again.

At first when they heard the sirens of the Guardians crying towards them, the sound was meaningless and could not reach them. But force of habit is strong, and suddenly the sound spelt fear and sent them running for shelter. Some of the little children screamed as they ran. Paul and Sharon hid, pressed side by side in the bushes at the base of the motorway wall. They watched as the van hurtled through the gap between two of the substandard blocks and bumped at full speed over the rough ground towards the fire.

Before the screech of its brakes had died away the rear doors had flung open and a dozen or so Guardians leapt in turn to the ground and jogged rapidly into formation. Then, like creatures in a dream, they began to move forward in a long straight line. Their white uniforms gleamed in the dark. Their hugely helmeted heads lent a menacing deliberateness to all their movements. Their breathing crackled viciously in the microphones set into their visors. The beams of their electric torches stabbed the ground. When they reached the fire one of them raked it with a fire extinguisher and it went out immediately.

Now, surely, they would move forward again towards the wall and the bushes, stabbing methodically through the thin refuges with their torch beams until they pried out the crouching forms. Paul's heart beat as if it would choke him. But it seemed the Guardians were not disposed to search thoroughly. They bounced their torch beams at random across the ground and up to the back of the blocks, catching white staring faces at the darkened windows that flinched away from them and vanished. A voice, cracked and mechanised by its microphone, gave an order. Instantly the van engine roared and the van reversed wildly up to the road. The Guardians formed up again and trampling over the ashes marched after it. The van doors opened and swallowed the white figures one by one.

Relief was instant and overwhelming. Although they stayed hidden for a while longer in case the van should circle around and return, it now seemed a game to be crouched among the grimy bushes almost within hearing of each other's heartbeats. Once, while they waited, Paul pressed his lips to Sharon's hard warm mouth, and smelt the bonfire in her hair. It made him entirely happy. When the siren had faded into the distance and the little children run off at random, they rose too and walked in silence, hand in hand, back to the block of flats. At the door they formally relinquished hands without looking at one another. They went up the stairs and into the flat.

He would have left at once, wanting to be alone and

to recall the fire while he could, but Sharon said in a flat practical voice, 'You can't go home with your shoes like that. Your mum would want to know why.' He waited then in his stockinged feet while she wiped away the ashes with a rag and rubbed polish into his shoes. Mrs Willmay slept in her creaking chair. Her head had lolled to one side in the moment of giving way to sleep. She provided them with an excuse for their silence, when the transition from the wild night to the placid room was too abrupt for any words. The two younger children came in with the same quiet satisfied air and sat at the table staring at Paul. The boy with awe. The pretty, irreverent little girl poked her head under the flap of the plastic tablecloth and giggled at the sight of his socks. Sharon brushed solemnly at his shoes as if she were giving a demonstration.

When they were to her liking she slid them across the floor towards him and clinked the kettle noisily on the stove. He wondered if she hoped to wake her mother, for she turned and looked sharply at Mrs Willmay, but she slept deeply on. The children watched her too.

'When does Mum get her Drink?' the boy asked.

'Later,' said Sharon irritably. More mildly she said to Paul, 'Mum says would you take her books back?'

'Yes, of course.' He knew he must go, but he did not hurry. It was strange to be present while the Drink was prepared in someone else's home. As he stooped to tie up his laces he heard her pry open the tin and tap the fine orange crystals off the measuring spoon into the children's mugs. She was pouring out hot water. The smell of the Drink was delicious in the room. He felt the measure of the walk in the cold before he would be home, before his mother would prepare his Drink for him.

Sharon set the two steaming mugs on the table. 'Now drink it nicely,' she said. 'Like Mum taught you.'

'To the future,' they chorused. 'To the future. To the future.' At first the little girl giggled helplessly as she sipped, but soon she grew quiet.

'Aren't you having any?' he said to Sharon as she handed him the books.

'Later. When she does.'

'Goodbye then.'

'Goodbye.' He wondered whether she would come to the door with him, but she leant back almost defensively against the stove.

'I'll let myself out, then.'

'Yes,' she said.

But as he was crossing the lobby to the outer door she leant over the stair rail and called down the lift shaft, 'See you tomorrow.'

'Yes,' he called back. 'Tomorrow.'

He was pleased to think that he would see her tomorrow, but he knew that by then the time for fires would be gone. The day after that he would lose the fire, except for what he might retrieve of it in writing and hide away. Even so it would shrink. He might read it again and again as he had the description of the other fire, but always what he read about had happened to someone else. Someone who had once been himself but whom he no longer knew.

He resolved to write again about this second fire. There was a piece of paper under the string that tied the books on which was written in a large bold hand, THANK YOU BUT NO MORE BOOKS. ELLIE WILLMAY. He slid it out as he walked. The back of it was blank. He would try again. This time he would describe the flames more accurately so that nothing of them should be lost. Nothing lost matters. But it did matter. While he could still see it as it was, knowing that he must lose it, it mattered most of all. It tormented him.

Don't hold onto it then, he told himself. *Nothing can be done. Don't try to write it down. Forget now before you must. Get home. Get home. Get home.*

But hurry as he might, it took a good half hour to reach the boundaries of his own Estate, and twice during that time he heard the sirens wail from different directions. It seemed, too, that a thin smell of fires was in the air, but that he might have imagined, for the smell also clung to his hair and clothes and filled his throat. He looked at his watch. It was only eight o'clock. There would be time for a bath before they shared their Drink and sat to dinner. *Get home,* he said to himself. *Get home. Get home.*

'You'll not be going out again tonight,' said his father.

His tone was cautiously balanced between order and entreaty. He waited for Paul's reaction to decide which line to take. His gran sat in her chair, watching him without seeing.

'Look at me,' said Paul. He wore his dressing gown which was suddenly too small for him. His short, washed hair lay in a darkened mat on his head. His ankle bones shone hot and pink over the sides of his long slippers. All traces of the fire were removed.

Far below in the street a siren shrilled and faded.

'It's no night to be out,' said his father.

'No,' said Paul. He went and drew the curtains without looking out.

'Drink time,' called his mother in a bright voice that shook off with an effort the cares of the kitchen. She carried in the tray of steaming mugs and the little bottle.

'I'll do Gran,' said Paul. He knelt and slid his arm gently behind the brittle shoulder blades and held the bottle to her lips.

'She's been as good as gold all day,' said his mother fondly. 'No trouble at all, have you, dear?'

'To the future.' They drank. 'To the future.'

But afterwards in his room, the fire became real to him again. He wrote on the back of Mrs Willmay's note in close straight lines what the flames had looked like, about their strength. He knew the extent of their strength, he wrote, because he had felt them in him. He had given his own unwanted strength to the flames. If only they were strong enough.

When he read it again he did not understand that last sentence and would have crossed it out, except that it seemed a waste of paper to do so and the words, having flown into his head from somewhere, must have some meaning and should be preserved.

CHAPTER SIX

IN THE MORNING the first thing he did on waking was to draw back the curtain over the window by his bed and read by the thin dawn light what he had written the night before.

He puzzled again over those words in his own handwriting, questioning whether the flames had been strong enough. Strong enough for what?

He lay back and watched the sky. Small lemon-coloured clouds trailed in soft mounds from beyond the sharp concrete edge of the next dwelling block. As he watched, the light intensified and blazed. It was the sun gleaming now on all the glass-fronted balconies, devouring with its brilliance a jagged hole in the straight line of the building. Then it sprang free. He looked at his watch. It was one minute past seven o'clock. He switched on the MEMORY. He learnt that it was Tuesday, November 6th. He turned his paper over and wrote in the gap above Mrs Willmay's large writing: Tuesday, November 6th. Sun rose 7.01am. He switched on the button marked *Daily Programme.*

He must go to school.

Words flickered on the screen. WELFARE AMENDMENT WORK TEMPORARILY SUSPENDED DUE TO DISTURBANCES ON THE ACKROYDEN ESTATE. CONTINUE TO RECORD DAILY NAME AND ADDRESS OF CLIENT AS CONTACT WILL BE RESUMED IN NEAR FUTURE.

He switched over to *Record*, and recorded Mrs Willmay's name and address while they were still clear in his mind. He thought it wise to record also a message to himself to return the books to Dr Palmer, and to dictate into the MEMORY Mrs Willmay's message, THANK YOU. BUT NO MORE BOOKS.

Then he lay back in bed and watched the sun through dazzled eyes across which his lashes lay like shining bars. He smelt porridge and heard his mother singing in the kitchen with all the joy of a newly discovered world.

On Wednesday morning he took the three books to the Special Investigations clinic. The corridor was crowded with boys, some his own age, some younger. They sat dejectedly in a line of moulded plastic chairs. Where the chairs ran out, a few more stood slouched against the wall.

Paul walked past them to a receptionist sitting at a desk in a white uniform.

'Have you an appointment?' she asked out of an impassive face.

'No,' said Paul. 'I don't want to see the doctor. I'm just returning Mrs Willmay's books.' He set them on the desk.

The nurse accepted him now, even allowed her face to brighten.

'Was there a message?'

'Yes. She said to thank you very much, but really she'd rather not have any more books for a while.'

The nurse laughed kindly. 'Oh she always says that. You'll get used to her. She loves reading really. It helps her when she can't sleep. She's a nice person, isn't she?'

'Yes,' he said. Monday, Tuesday, Wednesday. She was a shadow to him already, held only by the thread of her name and message, but he had a feeling that he had liked her.

'I always try to look out something a little out of the way for her.' She reached under the desk and drew out another pile of three tied together with string. The top book was covered with a piece of paper on which was written Mrs Willmay's name and a message, perhaps from the friendly receptionist. *Hope you find these interesting. They are all favourites of mine.*

A naked bulb set above the doctor's door flashed red and let out a fierce buzz. No one moved. 'Come now,' said the nurse. 'It must be one of you.' She took up a bundle of papers held by a metal clip and began flipping through them as she walked past the waiting chairs. Then abruptly she stopped and hurried back to her desk calling over her shoulder. 'It's you, Benson. You know perfectly well. And don't keep Dr Palmer waiting.' She reached out to the pile of books that Paul had brought and slipped them quickly out of sight into a drawer.

'There wasn't anything else was there?' she said impatiently.

Paul hesitated. In the half minute that the two piles of books had lain side by side, he had glanced automatically at their spines and seen that they were identical. The same three books again.

'I can't promise that she'll read them,' he said.

'You'll see. She won't be able to resist a good new read when she sees one.'

'You're sure they are the right books?'

'Yes. Positive. Why shouldn't they be?'

On the following Monday morning the MEMORY informed Paul that in payment for a wrong-doing he was to do two hours welfare work after school with a sick woman called Ellie Willmay who lived at 36, the Substandards, on the Ackroyden Estate. He was to take her three books.

He sat up in bed, drew back the curtains and spread on the blanket the pieces of paper on which he had written. On the reverse of one of them he found the same address. He had been there before then.

He leant his arms on the windowsill, the wrist with his

watch uppermost, and waited for the moment when the sun burst its way through the edge of the neighbouring block. On the note signed by the same woman, Ellie Willmay, he wrote: Monday, November 12th. *Sun rose at 7.12am.* He studied the column of figures he had already recorded on the paper. It had risen two minutes later than the day before and four minutes later than the day before that. And in the evening it set earlier and earlier. It was shrinking, dying. It was his secret, stolen day by day by means of the pencil and paper. It lay on his heart like a weight. The sun was warm on his face. It looked alive, but it was dying.

All day while he was at school, poring over statistics and projections, he forgot about the sun and lost himself in the abstractions of Futurism. But afterwards, climbing the hill towards the Ackroyden Estate, he watched for the exact moment of the sun's disappearance behind the wall of tower blocks. He would keep it in his mind until he was safely home and could record it then.

He walked along the central street of the Estate until he came to the far end. Then he took the perimeter road until he came to the gaunt substandard blocks. He studied lists of numbers on the boards by the entrances. Number 36 was a first floor flat. He ran up the stairs, looked along the landing until he found it and rang the bell. A moment later the door was opened by a girl. Tall, fifteen or so, with fair hair. She stood in the doorway, staring with wide direct eyes that seemed to require something of him.

'I'm from the welfare,' he said. 'I've some books for Mrs Willmay.'

Then, like the contracting lens of a camera, that strange look shut away from him. 'Come in,' she said shortly and stepped back to let him pass down the narrow passageway. 'It's the second door on the right.'

'Thank you.'

'Mum,' she yelled past him. 'It's a boy from the welfare.' It was as if she mocked him.

He pushed open the door and found himself in a crowded kitchen. The girl slipped behind him into the far corner of the room and leant with her back to the cooker, clutching her arms about her as if she were cold.

Two women sat side by side at a square table that almost filled the room. One was abnormally blonde. Hair that was almost white hung in stiff hanks on either side of an aging face. The face of the other woman was painted smooth and bright and crowned with a pile of crimson curls. They stared at him without a word.

Facing them, where the sun fell in a square patch through the window, a third woman, immensely fat, sat slumped in a basket chair. It was to her that he turned.

'Mrs Willmay?' It must be her. She looked so ill.

'Yes.' She roused herself, lifting her head to look at him. Then suddenly she smiled.

'Oh,' she said. 'Hello.' It was as if she thought she knew him.

He smiled shyly back at her. 'I've brought you some books.' He set them on the edge of the table beside her. The smile faded from her face. She was watching him suspiciously. Slowly, she reached out a heavy arm and, ignoring the note on the top, edged the pile of books around so that she could see the titles on the spines. She leant forward peering at them through the thick lenses of her spectacles.

Suddenly, without warning her voice rose to a shout of rage, 'Oh gawd, I told them no more books.'

A sickly bird in a cage on the windowsill flapped its wings so violently that he felt the draught on his cheek. He stood stiff with embarrassment, staring at the shouting woman.

The blonde friend had risen quickly from the table and catching hold of the hand on the pile of books began to pat it fiercely.

'Take no notice,' she said to Paul. 'She's not herself today.' But Mrs Willmay snatched her hand away and then dealt the books a blow with her arm that sent them over the edge of the table.

'Take the bloody things out of my sight!' she shouted.

The rage and violence of her behaviour were utterly repugnant to him. He knelt quickly to pick up the books. He wanted to be gone. The blonde woman knelt beside him saying anxiously, 'She's had a bad night, hasn't she, Rose? This isn't her, is it?'

'Never,' said the red-haired woman. 'She's not herself today.'

'She's very ill, you know,' Jeanie whispered in his ear. 'It's the drugs they give her make her act like this. It's not her. You won't say anything?'

Her anxiety confused him.

Who would I say anything to? What would I say? He felt too uneasy to ask. He picked up the books and held them in his hands, looking at the titles. He retrieved with effort the clinic, the hard bright voice of the nurse saying, '*You'll see. She won't be able to resist a good new read when she sees one.*' The identical pile of books.

Mrs Willmay lay back in her chair panting, glaring at him as if she hated him.

'They're the same books,' he said to her. 'Aren't they? The same books you had before.'

'You bloody know they are,' shouted Mrs Willmay. 'They're always sending the same bloody books over and over again.'

'It must have been a mistake. She didn't mean to. She was quite kind. She said she liked you.'

But nothing could stay the shouting voice. 'They pretend they're different, but they're always bloody the same. They think they'll catch me out. That's what they're after. They're trying to catch me out. But they won't,' she shouted at him. 'They won't!'

She stopped only because the effort had become too

much for her. She lay back in the chair again, panting and turning her head this way and that so that the wickerwork creaked in the breathless room.

Then the woman called Rose lowered her elaborate head into her hands and began to weep noisily.

'Oh gawd,' said Jeanie. 'What's going to happen now?'

'Nothing's going to happen,' said the girl desperately from her corner. 'He won't tell.' She turned her back on them as if that were an end to it and began to move the pans noisily on the stove.

But Jeanie was not done. 'How'd you know he won't tell, he's from the welfare, isn't he? They're all the same. All down like a ton of bricks on people like her. It's not as if she could help herself,' she shouted at Paul. 'It's not as if she were doing anyone any harm.'

He heard himself shout then, to his surprise, to his shame. 'What harm could I do her?'

The girl, without turning around from the cooker, said, 'If you tell them that she knows she's read the books before, they'll know her mind isn't working properly. They'll take her away.'

'I wouldn't tell,' he said. 'I've nothing against her. I don't even know her.'

Then Mrs Willmay's voice broke upon them as calmly as when she had first welcomed him. 'It's not his fault.'

'That's what you think, love,' said Jeanie. 'But you don't know. For all you know they might have sent him to spy on you. It makes you sick. He's just a boy.'

'It's a sick world,' said Rose wisely. She lifted her painted grief-stricken face on which, to his surprise, Paul could see no trace of tears. 'Isn't it, Ellie, love? Leastways, it isn't the world that's sick, it's the people. Isn't that so, Ellie? It's the people that's sick. Spying on one another. Telling the authorities. They're sick-minded people today. That's what I say. Sick-minded they are. Aren't they?'

'It's nothing to do with him,' said Mrs Willmay with the same steady conviction. 'He's all right.'

'Do you know me?' Paul said to her. 'Have I been here before?'

'Yes, love,' she said kindly. 'You'll have forgotten, but you used to come a few days ago. It wasn't your fault about the books. You weren't to know.'

He sat down then in relief on one of the benches with his back to the hostile women, trying to explain to Mrs Willmay. 'I thought they were the same books, but the nurse said they were different. She said she'd chosen them specially.'

'Yes. She would,' said Mrs Willmay. 'They know I used to love to read. They're just trying me out.'

He said, 'If I told them anything about you, I wouldn't know that I had.'

'You didn't tell them. They'd have been round here by now if they knew anything for sure.'

'That's true,' said Jeanie. 'That's true. They'd have been round, if they'd anything on you for sure.'

'They won't do anything,' said Mrs Willmay. 'You'll see. It's too much bother. Don't you worry, love,' she said to Paul. 'You'd have told them by now if you were going to. I'm not bothered by you. They only sent you here in the first place because you were a wrong-doer. You can't really be one of them.'

'Anyway,' he said sadly, 'I'll forget.'

'Yes. You'll forget. It makes it simpler for you really if you just forget.' She was quite composed now. She gave him a list of tasks to do and he recorded messages onto the MEMORY for her, as she seemed oddly confused as to how to work it.

When he left he picked up the books without asking her and put them in his rucksack. Sharon, on her mother's orders, showed him to the door.

'When I came,' he said, 'did you know me?'

She looked at him steadily in the light of the passageway. 'I've never seen you before in my life.'

He continued to come every day after that, and the Willmays began to take on a steady existence in his mind. They accepted him, and he was of use to them, especially over the working of the MEMORY. He was aware that they did not entirely trust him, that there was something about them that he did not know or had lost, but whatever it was he could not have wanted to preserve it, because he had written nothing of that nature on his worn scraps of paper. It might, he supposed, have something to do with their keeping the wretched parrot which he knew the Estate Council would not allow.

The only thing that he continued to record was the rising and setting of the sun. The one he recorded when he woke, the other on his walk to the Ackroyden Estate. And as the weeks went past, his solitary knowledge that the sun was shrinking, perhaps dying, exceeded his sorrow at the gradual decline of Mrs Willmay. Perhaps it was more real to him because it was possible to measure it and study every day the growing column of figures with their proof of regular decay. Mrs Willmay was better some days than others. Indeed, on the days when she seemed noticeably worse, Jeanie and Rose seemed loudest in their insistence that she had had a much better night or that she looked far more like herself, though all of them had lost any sense of what 'herself' had been.

He was scarcely aware of the day – he made no record of it – that she finally took to her bed, and no longer came into the kitchen. He saw her less frequently after that. He gathered from Rose's gossip pitched above the roar of the vacuum cleaner and through the cigarette she kept bobbing at the corner of her mouth, that the nights were very bad. That, poor soul, she needed to sleep when she could. It seemed that she had dreams, sometimes two or three in a night, causing her to wake and cry out. Sharon was often up with her, and sometimes he would see neither of them because they were sleeping, and do his chores to the sole accompaniment of Rose. But perhaps the next day he would come and find the bedroom door ajar, Rose and Jeanie sitting by the bed. 'Come in,' Mrs Willmay would call out to him.

One day she and Sharon were alone sorting through photographs. 'That's Mum before she was ill,' Sharon said to him with a shy pride. He took the scrap of card in his hand, and studied it. The photograph showed a strikingly handsome woman, still young, with a long switch of hair tied severely back, smiling up at him. He stole a glance at the woman in the bed, cropped hair, puffy features, her thick spectacles pushed awry as she leant back on the pillows. He could not have heard right. It could not be the same woman. But he admired the photograph and placed it carefully back in the biscuit tin although some instinct warned him it belonged in the paper-shredder.

The following day he thought of the photograph uneasily. People were what they were. It was wrong surely to claim that they had once been someone else and to keep from the paper-shredder proof that this was so. He felt relief when Rose met him at the door and said there was nothing for him. On the next day there was nothing but a feeling that something had been amiss. On the next, the incident was gone without trace from his mind. Mrs Willmay was what she had always been, a fat sick woman in a bed.

CHAPTER SEVEN

EACH MORNING HE laid his watch on the windowsill of his room, and timed the moment at which the sun gnawed a fiery bite out of the sharp straight side of the neighbouring flats. Each evening, walking from school, he watched it again drop out of sight behind the towers of the Ackroyden Estate and noted the time. Each morning it rose a few minutes later, each evening it sank earlier.

No one commented on this. The MEMORY, which must have known, being all-knowing, gave no warning. Paul himself found it quite impossible to share with anyone the thing that most occupied his mind. For another part of him continued just as he always had, woke each morning with a sense of wellbeing, loved his family and his Estate, turned to the MEMORY for information about the coming day, continued to go to school, and then on to the Ackroyden, differing in no way from thousands upon thousands of others, except that in his possession were several scraps of paper which he carried about with him now, anxiously transferring them from pocket to pocket until with wear and constant folding the paper was as soft as cloth and the writing almost illegible. Still, it excited and comforted him to read about the two fires and the part he had played in them. He had done what he could. Now he could only watch and record.

On December 22nd the MEMORY announced the winter break, five days in which double rations of the Drink would be dispensed and no work done. Families were advised to stay together in their homes. Only essential information about the nature and place of work to return to should be recorded that night. The rest might be wiped away. A new beginning would be made, the MEMORY promised, when the winter break was over.

Paul should have been overjoyed at the prospect, but renewed anxiety beset him. That day the sun rose at 8.04 and sank at 3.54, the shortest time yet. Then on December 23rd, the first day of the winter break, it rose at 8.03 and sank at 3.55. He studied these figures for a long time and compared them with the others. He scarcely dared to hope that the situation was permanently changed. On the 24th and 25th the same pattern repeated itself. On the 26th he recorded 8.00 in the morning. An immense relief filled him. The sun had recovered. It was growing strong again.

He had been excused his welfare duty over the five days of the winter break, but had carefully recorded on the night of his last visit the name and address of the flat and the date on which he should return. That morning, seeing the sun red and recovering, he decided suddenly to go and see this family and share with them his sense of joy and release before they became total strangers to him. To express it, even to feel it, in his own home seemed a dangerous thing. It had no place there.

Accordingly he switched on the MEMORY, dialled his identity number, touched the retrieval button, then, to refresh his mind, spelt out QUERY: NATURE OF WELFARE AMENDMENT. There was a pause. Then the screen spelt out: INFORMATION NO LONGER RELEVANT. AMENDMENT TERMINATED ON DECEMBER 25th. He was to attend Dr Palmer's surgery that afternoon for further instructions.

He felt a sensation of blank fear. Dim awareness that the other place existed was still with him. He had a strong instinct that he wanted to be there. A name, Wilton, Wilmott, was nearly retrievable, but the number and exact whereabouts of their home was gone. For comfort and strength he drew out his paper, and there on the back he found written in ink, a name, an address, the instructions that he had for some reason failed to destroy.

He did not tell his parents where he was going, merely that he was going out for a walk, and though he saw in both of them an intensity of glance and heard hesitation in their voices, neither of them questioned him, only watched him anxiously as he took his jacket and went out of the door.

As soon as he was in the street, he allowed himself to feel the full extent of his release and happiness about the sun. Any uncertainty about the people he was going to visit was consumed by it. He began to sing, holding up his face so that the sun shone fully on it. He turned towards the Ackroyden and saw the multitude of glass windows flashing in the cold bright light, knowing that the sun had triumphed and set out as he was doing with a high confidence on a new journey, gathering strength as he went instead of losing it.

No one noticed him. The streets were entirely empty and had a washed appearance as if a torrent of water had swept through them. Occasionally he heard a scrap of recorded music or a baby crying. An occasional hiss of tyres came off the motorway. Double rations of the Drink tended to make people drowsy and content to stay in the warmth of their homes.

Only once in all the long walk did he see a group of people approaching. Immediately, he stopped singing and walked more steadily. In a few minutes he passed a family warmly wrapped in new caps and scarves, wheeling an old lady. They smiled and nodded to him and he to them. He looked back and when they were at a safe distance began to run up the hill.

He crossed the Ackroyden without seeing another person. He seemed to know by instinct where to find the substandard housing area. Then he used the address on his piece of paper to find the block and consulted the number board to find out exactly which door to ring at.

The flat was on the first floor. He did not bother with the lift, but climbed the stairs. As he came onto the landing he was filled with an uneasy sense that all was not entirely as it should be. His mind struggled for what normal was in this place, but had lost it. Yet surely the bulging plastic sacks propped untidily by the wall and loosely tied so that one preposterously high-heeled shoe protruded from the top spoke of some failure or surrender in life waiting to be removed and hidden.

When he knocked at the door he found that his fist had pushed it partly open. Then as he pushed it further it wedged against a stack of cardboard boxes piled with saucepans and coat hangers and dented lampshades. There had been a sudden dismantling of lives that alarmed him.

He called out, 'Hello, is anybody at home?' but there was no clear picture in his mind as to who would come to his call.

A woman's voice answered, 'Who's that?'

'Paul, Paul Simonds,' he called into the ruined passageway.

'And who the hell's that?' said the voice. It was making its way towards him. A little dumpy woman stood in the passage with long thick blonde hair framing an old face, all swollen and reddened with weeping. He knew when he saw her that she was not the person he had expected.

'Where's the lady who used to live here?' he said.

'What's that to you?'

'I've come from the welfare to help her.'

'And what are you going to do to help her now, bloody welfare?' She took a step or two forward, staring at him. 'I know you,' she said. 'I've seen you somewhere. Do you know me?'

'I've seen you. Here I think.'

'I'm Jeanie, her mate.' She began to cry.

'What's happened to her?'

'She's gone.'

'Gone? But she was all right.'

'All right! Maybe she was when you last saw her, but in the end she was raving. She was only kept alive on drugs, you know, but in the end they couldn't do a thing for her. Even the Drink. Up half the night with dreams. All the shrieking to take the dreams away.' She fastened her hair over her ears, shaking her head from side to side as if the sound still tormented her. 'I couldn't listen. I had to go and leave her to Sharon. Things no child ought to hear. Some of it's still with me. It'll go tomorrow, thank gawd, I couldn't live with that. Terrible!' She turned away from him as she spoke and moved distractedly down the passage.

He knew that there was danger of contamination here,

that this woman was bent on telling him what he ought not to hear. Still, as he followed her down the dark passage, he felt compelled to ask, 'What things?'

'Terrible things. Things her grandmother had told her.' She opened a door and he followed her into a kitchen. There she turned to look at him and said in a shocked and lowered voice, 'Her gran told her that she had killed a bird and eaten it. It was horrible.'

'Yes. Horrible,' Paul echoed. For a moment he felt the same disgust, but his mind, better trained, resisted the obscene dream and discarded it before it took hold. He looked around the kitchen without recollection. The shelves by the cooker were stripped bare. Only a row of mugs still hung on hooks from one of them. A large cardboard carton was on the table filled with crumpled paper. Children's drawings, cardboard boxes glued together at school. There had been children. On the windowsill there was a bird in a cage. He knew he had seen that before. It disturbed him. It should not have been there. There was something wrong with it. 'What happened then?' he said to Jeanie.

'It was that Rose that told them,' she said bitterly. 'Would you believe it? Pretending to be her friend, like that. Saying she'd do anything. She told the authorities. That's what she bloody did. They came and took her away.'

'Where to?'

She shrugged. 'One of those centres where they take

people like that. They said it was hopeless. That she'd never come back.'

'And the children? There were children, weren't there?'

'Yes,' she said. 'Oh they're all right. You know kids. They'll have forgotten all about her by tomorrow. They're in the Home on the Estate. Sharon's allowed to stay with them for a day or two.'

She began to take the mugs from their hooks and set them on the table. *Sharon*, he thought. *There was a girl called Sharon*. He knelt on one of the benches drawn up to the table and looked more closely at the bird. It shuffled to and fro on its perch with grey clenched claws. Its wing feathers would not lie flat, but gaped untidily showing grey skin between. The head was hunched into its neck. A white film of skin blinked slowly up over its dull eye. It was not well. It irritated him that it should be so poor and sickly when the sun shone into its cage. He did not like the sun to have contact with it.

'I don't know what to do with that gawddamn parrot,' Jeanie was saying. 'I've all this to see to. They're moving in a new family on Monday. Oh gawd,' she said, suddenly sitting down in a wicker chair. 'I never thought to see her give way like that. I always thought she'd hold it off. Like she said she would. And then it came breaking through. All the things they tell us are lost. They weren't lost in her, poor soul. They all rose up to get her and what hope had she?'

He would have liked to say something to comfort her,

but all the time she spoke he was distracted by the presence of sunlight in the room. It fell through the window, a bright parallelogram flung across the stained table top, but it was marred by the narrow stripes cast by the bars of the cage and the hunched shadow of the bird. *It ought to be moved away from there*, he thought. *It ought not to be allowed to go on like that. It ought to be put down.*

'They'll do something for her at the centre,' he said. A kettle and a tin teapot were left by the cooker. Without asking, he made Jeanie a mug of tea and sat down at the table opposite her, automatically sweeping into his hand crumbs fallen at some unsuspecting meal before disaster came. She told him again about the terrible fragments of nightmare that had risen up and attacked her friend.

'They wouldn't let the kiddies see her. They took her away in the ambulance. They never said where. Sharon carried on as if her heart would break. But she'll forget, tomorrow. There isn't long to go now.'

Repeatedly, as he listened, a flicker of brilliance drew his eyes back to the cage. A disc of mirror framed in pink plastic dangled by a chain from the bars. When the bird disturbed it, it caught the light and projected leaping sunspots on the ceiling.

'I suppose I shan't be coming back then,' he said. 'Shan't see any of them again.'

'Not much point,' said Jeanie. 'Still, it was good of you to come today.'

'Can I help you?' he asked, indicating the room with his eyes.

'You could take those boxes out. The rubbish will be here soon.'

'Don't they want any of it?'

'Oh the welfare give them everything new. It's a fresh start for the kids. Not for her, though. Not much of a bloody fresh start for her.'

It took him some time to drag the boxes out of the hall to the landing. When he came back into the kitchen it was cold. He was aware first of a current of cold air on his face. Then he saw that the window was open and the cage empty.

'Where's the bird?'

'I let it go,' she said defensively. 'I don't know what she kept it for, sickly little thing.'

'I'd have taken it,' he said.

'You should have said so.'

'I didn't know you were going to let it out like that. It'll just die, being in the warm and then out in the cold. It hasn't a chance.'

'Well, it's only a bird, for gawdsake. What do you want it for anyway? It'll only get you into trouble.'

'I don't care.' He did not know yet what he wanted it for, but he knew that it was necessary that he have it. 'Can I have the cage then?'

'Have what you like.'

The thought of such a sickly infectious thing released into the fragile sunlight alarmed him. There seemed no limit to the damage it might do. He went anxiously to the window. The sun, unimpaired, fell on his face, warm through the glass.

Below him he saw the broad unkempt slope that led down to the barrier wall dividing the Estate from the motorway embankment. The shadows cast by the substandard blocks were still bright with frost, but beyond their sharp edges the sun had burnt away all trace of it. Bottle tops and discarded cans glinted among the brown clumps of uncut grass. Where the grass had been worn away there were broad muddy patches where footsteps and the wheels of children's toys had made gleaming ponds and channels. The whole sordid scene was transformed by light. It dazzled him. He narrowed his eyes to hunt for the green feathers of the bird and the flash of scarlet, but they were nowhere to be seen. Only at the end of the slope, where a thicket of dingy bushes had been allowed to establish themselves untended at the base of the motorway wall, was there anywhere it might hide.

He took the cage down from the windowsill.

'You'll only get yourself asked questions, walking about the Estates with that thing. Why not just leave it?' She sounded impatient and he had no answer.

He held tightly to the cage. 'I'd best be going now,' he said.

'Oh do what you like then.' But she followed him to the door and seeing the boxes lined in the hall thanked him. 'She fed it breakfast food,' she called after him softly. 'I daresay that's what's wrong with it.'

Outside he turned at once to the back of the substandards. The sunlight was brilliant, but out in the air it had lost its warmth so that he was immediately anxious again. At first he could see across the top of the barrier wall to his own Estate. Then as the ground sloped down, those familiar towers slid out of sight. He was walking across the ground he had seen from the window above, imagining that at the same time he stood at the Willmays' kitchen window watching himself moving all alone with the cage in his hand across the rough grass, stepping around the muddy patches, all the time moving forward with a purpose at which he, the boy at the window, could not guess. He did not look back, but if he had, it seemed he would have seen his face quite clearly framed in one of the first floor windows, the face of the boy who felt brief sorrow over Mrs Willmay, and compassion for the dying parrot thrown out into a world it was too weak to cope with. He himself, walking rapidly over the hard ground, was someone quite separate who knew what he was about.

Passing the charred circle of a bonfire, he knew to lean down and choose a twig that had escaped the flames. The sun had triumphed. He held the twig at arm's length and lashed it this way and that. The smell of the bonfire was on

92

his hand. His mind felt tense and alert. He knew the bird would be in the overgrown bushes by the base of the wall. He beat the stick through the air and heard it sing.

He could see that a circle of stones had been laid around the fire, but that it had been broken into and scattered when the embers had been raked out. He crouched down, and laying the cage carelessly to one side, selected four stones, placing them one after the other in his right-hand pocket. He could hear footsteps behind him on the hard ground, but he did not turn around, although in his head he listened acutely, trying to work out how many pairs of feet he heard. When he reached out for a last stone, another hand, smaller, dirtier than his own, stretched into the circle of his vision. A little boy, not more than five, squatted beside him. Dark hair fell in a fringe to his eyes. He wore a dirty pink jumper darned here and there with other shades of pink and red. He stared at Paul unsmilingly, wanting to find from him what to do.

When Paul took the fifth stone, he took one too and stuffed it in the pocket of his shorts. Other boys appeared beside him, crouching in a ring around the dead fire, filling their pockets with stones, watching Paul for some sign of what to do next. Some were already armed with sticks, others selected theirs out of the embers. He could sense the tension and expectation amongst them. They, too, were about some business. They were watching him, waiting for some signal. He pointed to the sun with his stick, smiled and they smiled back at him. They all knew. They all rejoiced. He was not alone.

He raised his stick and shook it at the sun. They raised their sticks and shouted. He began to move, not directly to the bushes but first in the shape and track of the sun, around and around the fire. His arms were stretched wide, weaving and swooping as he ran with little steps. Sometimes his splayed fingers folded up above his head and beat down strongly on the air. Sometimes they fluttered. He was the great bird soaring to the sun. He was the little bird hopping and hiding from branch to branch. He was all birds, strong and swift in the new sun. He was going to kill the ailing bird, that threatened the universe.

He picked up his stick and moved forward. They watched him stalk, swinging from the hips, looking this way and that, stretching before him with his stick. They fell in behind him, swaying as he swayed, creeping when he crept, leaping when he leapt.

When they reached the bushes, they spread out without a sound, each staring at the confused pattern of leaves and twigs in front of him. The wall towered above. At the roots of the bushes lay an ancient residue of cans and plastic wrappings, for the operatives never penetrated to prune or clean here. The bushes smelt of age and dust.

They were all very quiet, listening for the flutter of wings.

'I heard it,' whispered a boy. 'It's over here.' The others grouped silently behind him, peering into the gloom and grime of the bushes. They could see the bird's pale green shape, hopping stiffly among the black branches at the heart of the bush. The leaves of each twig quivered at the tip as the bird left it.

'There,' whispered the boy. 'But I can't get at it.'

'Beat it out.'

They began to batter at the leaves with their sticks. A little boy, the one who had first joined Paul at the fire, grabbed at an overgrown branch and began to shake it with all his strength, so that it nearly swung him from the ground on its rebound. He did it again and again until what he was doing seemed to become a purpose in itself. The others stopped beating and watched him, rattling the branch, his small sharp face rapt with pleasure. Then, as he swung, he began to sing, clearly, intently, as if he were unaware of the troop of boys watching him. Each word was clear and loud. His slight breathlessness, the rattling of the dry leaves, failed to obscure them. An ancient voice sang through him.

'The wren, the wren, the king of all birds.
On St Stephen's day was caught in the furze.
We chased her up. We chased her down.
Till one of our little boys knocked her down.
'We drowned her in a barrel of beer.
A Happy Christmas and a Merry New Year.
Up with the kettles and down with the pan.
A penny or twopence to bury the wren.'

He sang it through twice. They listened in perfect silence, devouring the few words that had any meaning for them. He finished it for a second time and released the branch. It rattled back into place and was still. Then, faintly, Paul heard the panicky beat of the parrot's wings and a moment later it appeared, hunched on a branch over their heads, its head sunk in its sparse feathers.

They began to leap and reach for it with their sticks, chanting their own chant gleaned from the little boy's song.

'We chased her up. We chased her down.
Until one of our little boys knocked her down.
Up with the kettles and down with the pan.
Kill, kill, kill the wren.'

It fluttered feebly to a higher branch and sat there blinking down at them, flapping its wings spasmodically, too weak to fly. Too weak to live in the strength of the sun. No weakness must weaken that, when the sun's strength was so new and defenceless. The weak must die. The strong must triumph. It must be killed so that birds might be made strong again to fly in the strength of the sun. He felt the stones in his pocket and took one out. The others fell back, watching him, chanting in a whisper,

'Up with the kettles and down with the pan.
Kill, kill, kill.'

He drew back his arm and narrowed his eyes in the sunlight, and threw the stone as hard as he could. It struck the bird, but he did not kill it outright. It fluttered uncontrolledly to a lower branch. A salvo of other stones pattered into the leaves. It blundered again from branch to branch. They could reach it now with their sticks.

'But he killed it,' they cried, bringing it to Paul by its gnarled feet. He held his hands open for it. It lay between them, a wretched little thing, its broken neck lolling between his fingers and thumb, its feet clenched, its feathers battered. Thick grey shutters were drawn up over its eyes. He felt triumphant. Out of all of them, he had led the hunt and his stone had secured the kill. He had some string in his pocket. He held the bird in one hand, while he found it. One of the others held out a stick and he lashed the stiff bent feet to it and raised it on high. The boys raised a cheer. Someone had torn down some leaves and twisted them into a crown. He ran and leapt behind Paul until he finally reached it up onto the top of his head. Paul was running, holding the stick and the bird high, triumphantly towards the sky. They were running beside him, shouting and cheering and leaping up as if to grab at the bird and hunt it again. They ran the length of the ground behind the substandards and back again. Then they stopped at the place where the fire had been.

Paul lowered the bird into the hole they had dug. But before they buried it, each took a feather. Paul, the king, had first choice. He chose a red tail feather and would have stuck it in his hair had not the first cold caution breathed on him then and made him sit back on his heels and fold it carefully into his precious wad of paper.

When he looked up at the others kneeling round the grave plucking feathers from Mrs Willmay's parrot, he felt dazed and confused. They stood back to let him complete the ceremony, but he had little wish to see. What was left of the parrot suddenly repelled him. But the thing must be done. They waited for him. Without looking down he kicked the little pile of dirt over the body and then scraped with his shoe any of the loose earth left and trampled on it. They all joined him then, trampling and trampling, but the gaiety and triumph had gone, and in their place awe and sorrow had settled.

Paul found the cage lying on its side on the ground and wondered why he had ever wanted it. He set it over the grave and balanced on it his wreath in which he now felt foolish. The older boys began to shamble off. The little children, still excited, stayed by the grave, decorating the cage with leaves and scraps of brightly coloured plastic bags retrieved from the roots of the bushes. When Paul left, only a few of them still played, absorbed, gathering stones and placing them in a neat boundary around the edges of the cage.

He walked home with the sun overhead, hurrying so as not to be late for his mother's meal. The sun was safe. He had done what he could. He struggled in his mind to grasp what had actually happened to Mrs Willmay, whom tomorrow he would lose. She would be lost to her friend who had wept for her, and to the friend who had given her away to the authorities. Her children would lose her. She would be lost to everyone. But did that mean that she no longer existed?

One of those centres where they take people like that.

Did they take them there to die or did they live out some new existence? His mind was loud and authoritative: *Nothing lost matters*. He could not think above the noise.

But afterwards, in his room, he typed out on the MEMORY, QUERY: THE WHEREABOUTS OF ELLIE WILLMAY, and watched as the bright letters jittered across the screen: NO KNOWN PERSON BEARING THIS NAME EXISTS ON ANY OF THE INNER LONDON ESTATES. CHECK YOUR QUERY FOR FAULTY DATA, AND REDIAL CORRECT ENQUIRY. He switched off the MEMORY.

It was later that afternoon, as he waited in the queue of silent morose boys outside Dr Palmer's office, that there came to him suddenly and quietly, with no interference, the thing that most appalled him about Mrs Willmay's fate.

CHAPTER EIGHT

'WELL,' SAID DR Palmer. 'How did you get on with your welfare work?'

'All right,' said Paul. 'Only it's over, isn't it?'

'Yes,' said Dr Palmer. 'That was a pity.' His eyes above their lugubrious pouches pondered deeply upon Paul, but his voice was impersonal, as if Paul were only one in a roomful of students to whom he lectured. 'Do you know what was wrong with Mrs Willmay?'

'She was ill,' Paul said guardedly. He tried to make it sound like a question, but there were to be no answers. Only more and more questions.

'Would you say she was ill in her body or ill in her mind?'

'In her mind?' said Paul. 'There was nothing wrong with her mind.'

'Oh, didn't you think so?'

'No. No, I didn't.'

'You never noticed that she suffered from illusions?'

'She had bad dreams. At least Jeanie said she did.'

'Dreams, illusions – Jeanie would be the neighbour?'

'Yes,' said Paul. 'There's a difference, isn't there?'

Dr Palmer was directing at him a sad and knowing smile. 'That's a fine distinction,' he said. 'I'm glad you brought that up. We must talk about that some time. It's all a question of control of the mind. We did our best to help her control it, but in some cases we are powerless. We did our best for her. Did you never notice exactly what was wrong?'

'No,' said Paul.

'She couldn't block off the past. She was tormented by things that she had done long ago. Things she had heard about. Things that had happened to her. Most people – ninety-nine per cent of people – can be freed of that burden now, but she was one of the few unfortunates.'

'I don't see why she had to be sent away. She was quite harmless.'

'Why do you say harmless?'

'She didn't hurt anyone.'

'You think she was fit to be in charge of children?'

'Why not?'

'You surprise me,' said Dr Palmer, who, now that he spoke directly to Paul, no longer looked at him but considered intently the pencil which he held propped between the yellow-stained forefinger of either hand. 'I'd have expected from you, Paul, a more sympathetic grasp of this woman's plight, and of the predicament we find ourselves in, in dealing with such a case. It's more than a matter of just her own wretched past. It's the past of the world, of human society. If any recollection of the past time creeps in, the mind becomes contaminated, and with the close mother-child bonding that I think you'll agree was strong in Mrs Willmay's case, there's almost the certainty of contagion. We have to be so very careful where children are involved.' He smiled across at Paul. 'You've no way of knowing, but the past is dangerous, terrible; it must be kept out. You think we have always been as we are now, kind, quiet, law-abiding citizens, civilised. But what if that were quite a recent thing, a revolution brought about in modern times by a generation which had the incredible wisdom to see that technological advance had reached its zenith, and destruction lay ahead? Scientists already had the power to remove the individual memory, but it was not until a common memory bank could be perfected that the individual memory could safely be dispensed with. What followed we refer to as the Enlightenment. It has meant a rebirth of society, a new chance at perfection, just as the world was destroying itself. Before that the human race was degenerate, vicious, filled with guilt and jealousy and hatred for one another. They even killed animals. They even killed each other.' He broke off. 'Is there anything about your time at the Willmays you feel you should tell me?'

'Yes, Father,' Paul said promptly. 'I killed the parrot.' The words seemed drawn out of him by Dr Palmer's voice, which had taken on as he spoke the warmth and strength of a personal obsession. It oppressed and excited Paul to listen to it, although what was said scarcely penetrated. Such a past must be too remote to have any bearing on him. He felt uneasily that the matter Dr Palmer really intended to discuss had not yet been revealed. Besides, words such as jealousy, guilt, hatred carried no meaning for him. Only the emotion with which Dr Palmer had spoken them gave them any significance. Now his voice grew indifferent again.

'Killed it, eh? When was that?'

'This morning.'

'How?'

'I hunted it, Father, with sticks and stones, until it was dead.'

'And then?'

'Then I buried it.'

'You buried it right away? Just as it was?'

Paul nodded.

'Where?'

'Down behind the substandards on the Ackroyden.'

'And the feathers. What happened to the feathers?'

'I pulled one out.' He took it carefully from his pocket without revealing the paper and put it on the desk.

'And the others?' said Dr Palmer.

'The other feathers?'

'Yes. Where are they?'

'In the parrot, I suppose.'

'You didn't distribute them amongst the others?'

'What others?' said Paul. He felt as if he were being forced to run by the quickening pace of footsteps behind him in the dark.

'Don't fence with me. You know what others. The other boys.'

'There were no others.'

'Then who sang the song? You could not have done.'

How does he know? Paul thought. *How is it possible that he knows?* He said:

'What song?'

'The song about the wren. You see, I know. It would be very dangerous for you to delude yourself into supposing that I don't.'

'Then why do you call it a wren. It wasn't a wren. It was a parrot.'

'In the song it's a wren,' said Dr Palmer. 'How do you account for that?'

'I don't know about any song.'

'What did you feel when you found you'd killed it? It was you that killed it, wasn't it?'

'Yes. I don't know.'

'You don't know what you felt or you don't know which of you killed it?'

'I killed it. I killed it.'

Dr Palmer got to his feet and moved restlessly to the window. He stood propping his long arms on the sill, staring down into the street. Somewhere below, a siren wailed. The sound floated up out of silence. The sun had set without Paul's being able to note the time. When Dr Palmer turned back, the room had darkened. Lit only by the artificial light coming in the windows; his face was colourless and indistinct, but his voice had ceased to batter and had resumed its measured, even pace.

'Don't you think it was a rather savage thing to do?'

'It was permitted, Father,' said Paul.

'Who gave you permission?'

'No one, but it was permitted. I knew. It seemed the right thing to do.'

'Why?'

'Because it was old and ill.'

'Is that a good reason for killing things?'

'Sometimes, Father,' he said. 'Sometimes.'

'And this was one of those times?'

'It seemed to be.'

'I see,' said Dr Palmer. 'May one ask how you feel about that now?'

'It seems incredible, now.'

'And how do you think you'll feel about it tomorrow?'

'Tomorrow, the day after, I'll forget,' he said promptly, for he saw it still without wanting to, small, bedraggled, with a thick white film dragged up over its eye.

'And are you glad you'll forget?'

'Yes, Father,' he said. 'I'm glad I'll forget about the parrot.'

'Tell me,' said Dr Palmer. 'When you killed the parrot, were you, do you think, in control of your mind? Or would you say – however cautiously – something, or someone, was in control of you?'

The question confused Paul. 'It was right,' he repeated. 'It was right.'

'Who told you it was right? Everybody you have ever known would have told you it was wrong.'

'Just today,' said Paul. 'We needed to be strong. We couldn't afford to let the parrot live like that.'

The whirr of the tape recorder asserted itself in the silence.

'So there *were* more than one of you,' said Dr Palmer softly. He closed an open book on the table with a snap. 'I thought there would be. Well, no doubt I'll see them all in time.' He switched on a little desk light that shone brightly onto a pile of papers, causing Paul to blink. 'I have your school report here. It's very good. Very pleasing. The headmaster says you've been working very hard. Overworking, in fact. He says you need a break.

A complete rest. How do you feel about that?' Above the bright lamp Dr Palmer's face hovered in shadow. It waited there behind the gentle reasonable voice, watching Paul, who felt for the first time obscurely frightened.

'I don't want a rest. I like the work.'

'It's only a short break. It won't last for ever. You can retrieve anything you want from the school MEMORY. We'll have your home MEMORY fixed onto it. I spoke to your mother this morning. She's quite happy about it. All it means is that you'll spend the next few months at home, resting up. Then when the warmer weather comes, a fresh start.' The decisive, friendly tone, the frank smile with which he said this Paul recognised as signals of dismissal. He reached out for the feather.

'You still want that, do you?' said Dr Palmer. 'I hope in a day or two you'll have lost interest in it and have the sense to throw it away.'

Paul took the feather and put it in his pocket. He got to his feet and hesitated still by the desk. 'Would I be allowed pencil and paper?'

'Certainly, if you don't abuse the privilege.' He watched Paul for a moment and then he said, 'The sheets will be numbered, of course, and their destruction recorded by weight. It may seem petty to you, but you understand we have to be very careful about letting paper out of the controlled environment of school. It's tricky stuff. There's always the danger of contamination.'

By the door Paul turned back. 'There's something I wanted to ask, Father.'

'Yes, my son?' said Dr Palmer impatiently, without looking up. His hand had moved over to the button which ignited the red bulb in the hall. It paused, but hovered there.

'It's Mrs Willmay's children. They will forget her, won't they?'

'Yes, naturally.'

'Will she forget them?'

'No. She cannot forget. Nor would you be able to if you found yourself in her position. No provision is made at the centres for blocking memory. The people there have to do without. All drugs are withdrawn.'

'But Mrs Willmay was kept alive by drugs.'

'Was she? Who said so?'

'Everyone.'

'I doubt if I said that.' He pressed the button on his desk, and Paul could hear the loud buzz in the passageway.

'Turn on the light as you go, will you?'

Paul clicked the switch as he went through the door. Light filled the room behind him, but he did not look back at Dr Palmer, nor at the nurse at her desk in the corridor, nor at the waiting boys, one of whom shouldered past him at the door of the office. He went home. There was nowhere else to go.

CHAPTER NINE

THE PLAYING FIELDS beyond the sports pavilion were covered with a durable artificial grass which had been expensive to lay, but had saved the Estate countless time and money ever since. Nevertheless, at the end of those fields nearest the centre of the Estate, opposite, in fact, to the entrance of the main shopping complex, was a small caged enclosure containing living grass, a pond and a few trees.

It was kept because for some reason it contented the old ladies during the period of temporary stress to which they were subject when the warmer weather arrived. This agitation in the spring had often been noticed in them, an inexplicable fretfulness, what seemed an effort at expression. It was distressing for the devoted women who cared for them, and anything that soothed it was officially encouraged. The Council therefore had constructed an elegant concrete platform around the outside of the high railings that surrounded the enclosure. Ramps led up to it at intervals so that the old ladies' chairs could be wheeled up to a vantage point in the sun. There were benches, too, on the platform and on the pavement by the railings where the younger women might sit together and chat, for they could see nothing special in the spring. The world renewed itself each day, not at one time of year more than another. Still, if the old ladies were content to stare by the hour at the life behind the bars, they were happy to sit and wait for them, their heads inclined towards one another, their bright bits of handwork spread on their laps, their fingers in a state of placid constant agitation.

On one of these benches as winter turned to spring, Paul would often sit. He was quite alone because the weather was still too cold for wheeling out the old ladies. He would stare fixedly between the bars of the enclosure as in a week or two they would. Had anyone been able to make this comparison, it would have surprised him that Paul, so young, should behave like the senile women. As it was, the computer technicians in the nearby office block, looking through their windows in the afternoon, recollected that someone had sat there the day before, and in the vague discontent that seemed to have crept over them as the days lengthened, wondered who he was, free to sit staring between the bars while they must stay shut away for another two hours, by which time the light would fail and the artificial light in some way spoil everything.

He came so regularly to the bench that the sight of him became quite familiar. He became someone whom these office workers knew, if only in the sense that on the late April day when he failed to appear and even the day following, a number of people working on that side of the block felt the uneasy, frightened feeling that comes with a sense of loss, when it is impossible to identify exactly what has gone. Some of them even checked through their desks to satisfy themselves that everything was in order. Others turned repeatedly to their office MEMORIES to reassure themselves that they had neglected none of the day's recorded tasks.

It was observed in one of these offices that a young domestic technician was twice found weeping at her work, but even if anyone had been capable of the highly complex and utterly useless feat of connecting these tears with the absence from a familiar scene of one of its elements, it would have aroused little interest. She was an odd unapproachable girl whom people tended to avoid. In any case, she herself disappeared the following day, and once the inconvenience of replacing her at short notice was over, she was immediately forgotten.

It had seemed to Paul as he went down in the lift from Dr Palmer's office that the exclusion from school would be intolerable, but of course it was not. Three days later he had lost everything but his family, his home, a red feather whose origin he could not explain, and several pieces of paper covered in his own handwriting. If it had not been for these he would have known nothing of his loss, but they provided him with some measure of it. They awed and frightened him. He knew that he had stolen these things from the MEMORY, but they were his, they had happened to him, and so, as he thought about it, he reasoned that the MEMORY must have intended to steal them from him. Not all that went into the MEMORY came out of it again.

He read the papers each day until the words were embedded in his mind, like his name, his address. He read them with disbelief, knowing them to be true. They spoke of a different existence of which he had no knowledge, yet he had watched the flames. He could not know it, but he must believe it. The name, written in ink, Mrs Willmay, he repeated again and again, like an invocation, feeling that at any moment it would disclose its true meaning. He stared at the red feather, but neither revealed anything to him at all. He ceased to record the rising and setting of the sun because he no longer feared for it. He recorded nothing else because nothing else seemed of any importance.

In the morning he went into his room and switched on the MEMORY. His own voice repeated the essentials of Futurism. Other voices dictated statistics of births and deaths. Without questioning whose voices they were or why he did this, he worked out prognostications, the number of school places that would be required (a steady decline), the increase in housing especially designed for the elderly. He worked for hours over meticulously coloured charts and graphs and then recorded them for the MEMORY on video tape.

NOW DESTROY ALL PAPER, the MEMORY's voice told him. THIS IS ESSENTIAL TO AVOID CONTAMINATION.

He fed the charts into the paper-shredder.

Between lunch and tea he went for a walk, never beyond the bounds of his own Estate, but combing it three hours at a stretch. Never had he known it so well or loved it so much. It took on an entirely new familiarity. Because he felt the need to possess it, he took care always to follow the same route so that one building rose behind or appeared beside another, in precisely the same procession of patterns as he moved. He began by climbing Santan's Hill, the highest point of the Estate, and studying the view to the south. He took another road down the hill, past the school. He had no recollection of ever attending it, but had come to know every detail of its external appearance. At the same time, the faces of the pupils that he passed each day as they came out and made for home took on an immediate impression of familiarity, but as people he had once known and worked with they were quite lost to him, and he to them. They passed one another without smiling or speaking, as befits strangers. Finally he would take a short cut through the shopping centre, pressing his way through the slow placid crowds who walked to and fro, staring at items with which they someday planned to elaborate their homes.

From here he made his way through swing doors into an empty concrete space where plastic bags scurried, prodded by the sharp spring air. It gave onto the road which skirted that same small enclosure preserved for the old ladies, and here he sat for a time on one of the benches set out for their keepers.

The trees inside this enclosure, although carefully pruned and swept up after, were left free of their individual cages. They had grown into quite different shapes to the correct lollipop forms of the caged trees on the pavements. At first he found them upsetting, deformed, their stiff motion in the wind uncanny. Then he made a discovery about them that utterly absorbed his attention. The trees changed.

He had chosen this bench because it was set opposite the tree closest to the railings, whose twig hands stretched nearly to the bars and even rattled along them if the wind were high. These twigs he watched intently day by day. He had not noticed before that trees changed. His span of memory was so limited that it could only encompass those minute changes that he had never before had time to examine.

Now, before the image of the brown swollen bud had

entirely faded, he saw break a jagged line of green, and while that image was still with him, he saw emerge the limp, sharply creased leaf. Before, the state of leaf and bud had each in turn seemed absolute; that one was a progression of the other astonished him. When the leaf was fully opened and ceased to alter noticeably, he lost hold of this fact, but an aura of excitement still hung about the tree, and kept him coming back to the same spot day after day.

One afternoon he noticed a jagged rent in the asphalt at his feet. A cleansing department van was in the street at the time and some operatives were employed in cleaning out the gutters under the observation platforms with their suction machines. It occurred to him that he should report the imperfection, but he hesitated, being unsure that the Cleansing and Hygiene Department dealt with such matters.

On the following day the rent in the asphalt was unrepaired. He sat on the bench, leaning over it, studying it. He could see that a little ridge of brown earth had forced its way up through the crack. He reached down, ran his finger gently along it and felt something firm in the earth. When he lifted his hand he had revealed the hard smooth tip of a green shoot. It should not be there. It had done damage to the Estate. He should rub it out with the heel of his shoe and try to force the asphalt level, but the more he stared at the green defiant speck, the more he was unable to destroy it. The tremendous drive and optimism that had strengthened it to disrupt the asphalt awed him. It had grown from below, fighting for light.

There was no one in the road. He knelt beside it, willing it to reach further, to live, wondering if it felt his presence there. When he heard the operatives' van at the end of the road, he felt afraid for it. It was in the wrong place. It would not be tolerated. He glanced quickly at his watch and noted the time, 3.47. If they came at that time today, they would come at that time every day. He hefted the bench by its arm and found he could move it quite easily. He looked up and down the road. No one was watching him. The schools were not yet out. He dragged the bench over to the crack so that it could not be seen from the road. Then he sat down placing his feet one on either side of it, guarding it.

The van swung into the road. A green-uniformed operative jumped out and a vacuum cleaner on wheels was lowered down to him. The van crept along the side of the pavement, its circular wire brush scouring out the gutters. The man with the vacuum followed along behind, sucking up the displaced dirt into the nozzle of his machine. Paul took off his jacket and draped it over the back of the bench. He stared over to the empty football pitch, listening to the scratching of the wire brush and the whine of the vacuum coming closer. He sat hunched over the plant as if he would defend it with his life. No need. The man and the machine went slowly past. He stayed on the bench until it disappeared around the corner of the road. Then he stood up, put on his jacket, and edging the bench a little closer, pushed the loose earth up around the shoot to hide its burning green. Then he walked home.

The next morning, for the first time, he found it difficult to concentrate on the statistics. He kept thinking about the plant, wondering how it might have changed, fearing that it had been discovered and destroyed. He timed his walk exactly so as to be at the bench a quarter of an hour before the operatives' van rounded the corner. The plant was there, visible now above the edges of the asphalt, displaying a fierce vivid green that became at once his pride and his terror. He wanted it to grow, but as it did it would become more and more conspicuous. He swung his jacket over the back of the bench and took from his pocket his statistical tables and waited, pretending to study, listening for the van. At exactly 3.47 it rounded the corner. He had known it would be punctual. He waited, holding the book open over the plant until they were gone.

He came the next day and the next. He had never believed that it could survive so long. He sat with the statistical tables open on his knee, pretending to study, but staring intently at the plant below the straight edge of the page. He had forgotten the first appearance of the shoot. It seemed that it had always been as it was now, a tall fragile thing. The stem was translucent. It seemed that he could see the liquid pulse inside it alive with the light captured from the low cold sun. He could have snapped it in his fingers, it was so fragile, but in its struggle to reach the light it had torn the asphalt and braved a hostile world. He bent his face closer to it and smelt its cold live smell. He wanted to speak to it.

On the very edge of his absorption he was aware of someone approaching, sharp footsteps slowing. The seat of the bench gave slightly. He glanced sideways, hiding the plant with his trouser leg, straightening a little so that his eyes were in line with his book. A girl with fair hair. Harmless enough. But it annoyed him that she sat there. He spread his knees wide, propped his elbows on them, held the open book in the basket of his big hands, looked blindly at the print, and quickly away from the girl to the end of the road where the van would appear.

All the time that he did not look at her, he was very aware of her. When she spoke he turned sharply. 'You come here every day, don't you?' She held her face towards him, tilted a little defiantly upwards so that the sun fell upon it and drew a thin line of light around the edges of her hair. Not an expressive face. Smooth skin laid on cheeks and forehead, no wrinkle, no movement. But she was watching him with unguarded expectant eyes. She frightened him.

He said cautiously, 'I came here yesterday and the day before. Maybe the day before that.'

She continued for an instant more to stare at him. Then

she drooped her head and began fumbling in a plastic bag on her lap with big clumsy hands. Her hair fell straight over her shoulder and hid her face like a curtain. 'Have a biscuit,' she said, holding out the bag without looking at him.

He thought it safer to accept. It made him uneasy to think that he had been watched. He feared for the plant.

'Thanks.'

There was silence apart from the sound of chewing inside his head. The girl behind her fall of hair nibbled the edges of her biscuit like a child trying to make it last. 'Have another,' she said.

'No thanks.'

She began folding and refolding the top of her plastic bag. Her words came timed to the movement of her fingers. 'I've watched you every day. I thought maybe you'd come to meet a lady friend.'

He snorted.

She looked at him again, not openly as she had at first, but seriously, with grey eyes as unrevealing as low cast cloud. She said, 'You're hiding something, aren't you?'

'You've seen it?'

'I saw it yesterday. After you went I came down and sat here. I saw it then.'

'Have you told?'

'No.'

He tried to think what it was she might want of him.

There was no reason to trust her, only the sudden awareness of his own isolation. He moved his leg away, revealing the plant. They both looked at it.

'Brave, isn't it?' she said.

'They'd kill it if they knew it was there.'

'Yes. Wouldn't they.'

'Do you know what it is?'

'Well, it's a plant, isn't it?' She began to talk rapidly like a child reciting its lesson, with a stiff little pride in what she knew. 'A tree is a plant, grass is lots and lots of little plants. Food is dead plants.'

'They'd kill it if they found it,' he said again.

'They're sure to find it in the end. I shouldn't fret over it if I was you.'

'They always come around about now.' He glanced to the end of the road, anxious suddenly that the van might have crept up on him unawares. No sign of it. He tugged his jacket into a better position over the back of the bench. His watch said 3.46. They heard it then. At exactly 3.47 it turned the corner. They listened while the van worked its way slowly towards them, he staring down at the column of figures in his open book, she twisting and twisting the corners of the plastic bag.

The van vibrated past. The operative passed so near that even above the sound of the mechanical broom and the vacuum, they could hear the metallic scrape of the nozzle as he moved it along the gutter behind them, and the scuff of his boots on the road. Now, surely, he had stopped and seen something, but no. The hum receded. He was moving slowly on. He was gone. They glanced at one another in unsmiling conspiracy.

'Well,' Paul said in relief. 'Well.' He doubled his arms behind his head, sunk his chin close to his neck and arched his back, stretching with pleasure. Then he snapped shut his book. The purpose of the day was over. He must go home. He stood up, laid the book on the bench seat, hauled his jacket off the back. The air was chilly. He was glad to pull it on. Automatically he felt for the little wad of paper in the lining. He picked up his book. The girl was watching him again. He felt uncomfortably that something more was expected of him. 'I must go,' he said, but he did not feel free to move.

She dusted imaginary crumbs from her skirt. 'I could come and sit here tomorrow if you like. They'd not get suspicious then. They'd think you'd come to meet me.'

He did not want her to come. The thought of having to talk to her while they waited weighed down on him. But he could see the truth in what she said. He daren't offend her.

'All right,' he said indifferently. 'If you want to.' He shifted the book from one hand to the other. 'Goodbye, then.'

'Goodbye.' As indifferent as he. But she turned sideways on the bench, watching him go. He hurried away from her. 'You don't know my name,' she called after him.

'Tell me next time,' he called out. 'Keep me guessing.'

'I'll guess yours.' She was kneeling up on the bench.

'You won't,' he called over his shoulder. He kept walking rapidly away, but all the time he strained to hear her answer.

'Paul,' he thought he heard. 'Paul.' It nearly stopped him. *That's what she wants me to do*, he thought. *Stop and go back*. He broke into a run and hurled himself with outstretched arms at the swing doors of the shopping centre. The noise he made drowned out all other sounds. He wanted to be home.

As soon as he was in the flat, the outside portions of his life were in some way destroyed. He could not believe them real. That night at supper, as he lifted the limp green food to his mouth, he struggled to remember the plant.

His father said in a hard probing tone, 'Is anything wrong?'

'What have I done?' Paul said. 'What have I done now?' He was aware that he had spoken in anger for no reason. Both his parents were staring at him aghast. He would build his anger then into something real and solid, so he persisted, 'What have I done?'

'Nothing,' said his father. 'You were just very silent.'

'Well I've nothing to say. I don't do anything. What am I meant to talk about?'

'You did something,' said his mother brightly. 'All morning in your room.'

'What did you do today, boy?' said his father. He was waiting, his big defenceless face turned towards Paul.

'I did some charts on geriatric housing units and fed them into the shredder.'

'Good,' said his father, beaming. 'Good for you, boy.'

CHAPTER TEN

THE NEXT DAY he saw the girl waiting there as he came through the doors of the shopping centre. She was wearing a little blue scarf tied over her head, entirely hiding her hair, so that he tormented himself as he walked towards the bench with the thought that she might turn out to be a stranger, hostile to the plant.

He began to hurry, almost to run. At the sound of his footsteps, she turned. The same girl.

'It's all right,' she said when he came closer. The plant still grew beside the bench. He took up his position, staring down protectively at it, shy with relief and pleasure. The van was not due for another ten minutes. They could not sit in total silence.

'Where do you live?' he asked.

'In the hostel. I work up there.' She pointed vaguely

up at the face of one of the administrative blocks behind them. 'That's how I saw you.'

'Typing?' Why had she come again?

'Cleaning.'

'Where are your parents?'

'Lost.'

'Oh,' he said. The minutes went slowly past. He listened for the van. He was sure she did not come for the sake of the plant. She looked for something in him that he was unaware of.

She said, 'Why don't you go to school?'

'I don't know. I work at home.'

'Do you like that?' She spoke as if he were a child, as if she possessed his answers already.

'I'm not bothered.'

When the van had safely passed, he got up. He felt he should have made more effort to talk to her. He wondered if she would come again. It occurred to him suddenly that she might have been sent to watch him, for she had known his name. Still, she had not betrayed the plant.

'What's your name?' he asked her. 'I couldn't guess.'

'Sharon.'

'How do you know mine?'

'I don't.'

'But you knew it last night.'

'No, I didn't. Why should I know your name?'

She's lying, he thought. *Why should she lie?* 'It's Paul.'

'Hello, Paul.'

'You'll come tomorrow?' He could not have said whether he wanted the answer to be yes or no.

'I'll see. Goodbye, Paul.'

The following morning he made no attempt to settle to his statistical work. Instead, he sat on his bed staring at his MEMORY. He tried to separate what he knew about it from what he felt about it. Every morning he dialled his code number and a voice instructed him what to do. The voice knew who he was by the code number. At night he dialled his number again and dictated into the MEMORY all that he needed to know for the next day. Not all of it was returned to him, so someone must be there. Someone decided what he could keep and what he must lose.

He had never confided much in the MEMORY. So far as he knew, his father scarcely ever used his at all, relying solely on the one provided by his office. But his mother shut herself in her room for an hour or more a day and talked to her MEMORY as if it were another human being. It was as much a daily part of her, and so as much a part of his awareness of her, as her name, her face. He got up and went slowly into the kitchen.

His mother stood by the stove shredding a cabbage with a knife. He found he had no way of talking to her about the MEMORY. He could not think how to begin. He lifted the lids one by one from a row of tin jars pushed against the wall. Each one had a different kind of dried bean stored in it. He stared at them moodily and rattled the lids as he replaced them.

His mother said, 'Why don't you go and have a talk with your gran? She's been ever so restless today.'

'What's the good?' he said. 'You can't talk to her.'

'Don't say that.' She turned around indignantly. 'You know she understands a lot of what we say. Just because she can't speak.' Her voice had become pitiful and she went back to her chopping.

'What's your code number?' he said.

'None of that,' she said crossly, with her back to him. 'We'll have none of that talk.'

'No, seriously.'

'You know I can't tell you that. There's some things have to be private.'

'I just want to know if mine's different.'

'Of course it's different.'

'Why?'

'Now, Paul.'

'No, I'm not trying to be funny. If I dialled my code number and asked it a question, and you dialled your code number and asked it the same question, would it give you the same answer it gave me?'

'It would depend on the question, wouldn't it?' She was evading him. He thought she did not know. 'It's the truth,' she said. 'You can depend on that, whatever it says it's got to be the truth. Besides, some things are private things.

All that's very private or else we'd talk to one another instead.'

He looked directly at her then. 'Does someone listen at the other end?'

'Now, Paul. That's nasty.'

Back in his room he dialled his code number, then he typed out: QUERY: IS ANYONE THERE.

No answer.

He thought for a moment. Then he dialled six digits at random.

QUERY: WHO AM I.

The letters jerked on the screen: THE PENALTY FOR IMPROPER USE IS DISCONNECTION OF THE MEMORY.

The girl was there that afternoon. He saw her in the distance and immediately walked more slowly, denying to himself that he had been afraid to lose her. She was sitting sideways on the seat, watching for him. She neither waved nor smiled, but waited until he was quite close. Then she began slowly to shake her head. He ran towards the bench, but realised then that it had been moved back to its original position. A little way from it the brown corpse of the plant lay sprawled on the crack it had made in the pavement. A white powder had been scattered all around it. Poisoned.

'I knew they'd find it,' she said. He felt she didn't care enough. He had hoped absurdly that it would survive. He didn't want to talk about it. The tight congested feeling in his chest must be anger. He did not know where to direct it other than at the girl who had found the plant before he had.

'Well,' he said. 'There's no point in sitting here then.'

'I'm sorry,' she said. 'Really I am.'

He got up and walked away without a word.

When he got home his mother was preparing supper. The smell of cabbage came through the closed kitchen door with the dull ring of metal pans as she shifted them about on the cooker. The old lady sagged in sleep by the electric fire. His father sat opposite, reading his newspaper. Soon his mother would bring in the Drink. That would make him feel more himself. He stood staring out of the window. The blocks of flats stood up against the evening sky like computer cards punched out into irregular patterns of light and dark. The artificial lighting had not yet come on. Between the flats and in the bare area by the football pitch, the early darkness had a hollow inviting quality. He wanted to go outside again and walk for a while. They would not want him to. They would argue with him if he mentioned it. Finally they would say it was not safe to be out at night. He could hear his father shift in his chair, and sensed that he wanted to talk, but was at a loss for something to say. He made no attempt to help.

When, a moment later, his father did speak, it was to say irritably, 'Why are you forever staring out of the window? There's nothing to see.'

His mother, as if she had been listening for the sound of voices, put her head round the door and said, 'Paul's been asking questions. You should have a talk with him.' She moved quickly out of sight behind the door, shutting it behind her. Paul turned into the room, propping himself on the warm radiator. His father had lowered the paper across his knees, but still held defensively to the edges of it. He said, 'What is it you want to know, boy?'

Paul said quickly, 'Why do they keep the trees in cages?' He could see that this was not the question his father had been expecting, nor was he to be hurried into an answer.

He let the paper slide to the floor, took up his pipe from an ashtray on the table by his chair. He brought out his lighter from his pocket and flicked it rapidly until it flared. Then, elaborately, he sucked down the flame into the tobacco as if he were performing some adult ritual from which Paul was excluded. It provided, too, for his speech being altered and his eyes averted as he said, 'Why do you call them cages? They're supports.'

'What do you mean supports?' said Paul scornfully.

'You know what a support is. It holds things up.' It was meant to be an end to the argument. He went back to fussing over his pipe. The old lady sighed and jerked in her sleep without waking. A speck of dust flared on the bar of the electric heater.

Paul said, 'Couldn't they stand up without them?' He could hear the disbelief in his own voice.

'Yes, of course they could, but they wouldn't keep their proper shape. They're bad enough as it is. Besides, it protects them!'

'From what?'

'People. They do, you know, at least some do. Hurt trees.'

'How do you know?' In the placid, insufficient room, his voice sounded accusing. He could see displeasure and uncertainty in the sucking movements of his father's lips about the stem of the pipe, and wondered, with a little quickening of excitement, whether it was possible to provoke him to anger.

But when his father spoke he had fallen back on the passionless tones of some office MEMORY. 'My department is responsible for the maintenance of trees as well as for other facilities on the Estate.'

Paul said stubbornly, 'But what would happen if the cages were taken away?'

'Why do you keep calling them cages? They're supports.'

'Well, if they were taken away . . .'

His father wouldn't let him finish. 'People would interfere with them.'

'In what way?'

'In lots of ways.' Each time they spoke their voices seemed to have climbed another step towards some dangerous exciting release. *He is angry*, thought Paul. *What am I saying to make him angry?* But he wanted it to go on.

'Could they move?'

His father's voice hurtled into the room, so that the placid air seemed shaken from wall to wall with his indignation. 'No, of course they couldn't move!'

The old lady twitched and started like a tiny child. All sounds stopped in the kitchen. The door handle rattled. His mother came in, looking from one to the other in alarm. 'What's the matter?'

'Nothing's the matter,' said his father. 'Paul's being stupid. That's all.'

'But Paul's not stupid. He's very clever.'

'He's being very stupid.' He was sullen to his wife, ashamed because he had shouted.

'What have you done?' she said sharply to Paul.

'Nothing.'

'He wants to know if trees would move, if their supports were taken away,' said the father, large again in his scorn.

'Of course they wouldn't move. You know that,' his mother said reproachfully to Paul. 'Trees don't move about.'

He nodded dumbly at her. He had quite lost track of the argument and what he might have wanted from it.

'They're only plants, love,' said his mother. She stood for a moment, watching him in bewilderment. Then she gave a little cry at some sound behind her and ran back into the kitchen.

Nothing had been resolved. As soon as she had gone

Paul began again in a vehement whisper, 'You don't know. You don't know why they are in cages.'

'I know they're a damn nuisance. I know they should be got rid of. I know the planning committee won't replace them when they die. If I have any say they won't wait for that. They're nothing but parasites.'

'They've a right to live. Why do you want to go around killing things?'

'Damn it, they're plants!'

'They're alive, aren't they?'

'Food is dead plants. I don't see you refusing food.' He got up violently from his chair and leant all his weight against the radiator so that it shook behind Paul's back. He shouted against the window glass, 'Why don't you do anything? Why are you always here staring out of the goddamn window?'

'I don't know,' said Paul. 'I don't know. I don't want to be here. I do what the MEMORY tells me.'

'So do I! So do I!' Each time he spoke he struck with the palm of his hands down onto the windowsill. 'But it tells me to work. Why doesn't it tell you to work?'

The old lady's cry silenced them instantly. The unaccustomed pitch of anger had finally dragged her up to the surface of sleep, and now she sat crouched in the chair, rocking herself to and fro, whimpering. Her bent hands groped convulsively on the blanket on her knees, like stricken creatures feeling about for shelter.

'Look what you've done,' said Paul's father. But the current was broken between them. His voice was shrunk to a whisper. Paul knelt beside the old lady and put his arms around her and rocked gently with her. His heart was beating rapidly. He could feel its beating pressed against the frail old body, so wrapped in shawls that it seemed to have taken on the soft yielding substance of the blanket. He felt frightened and infinitely relieved, as if he had stepped aside from a great danger. The anger was quite gone in him. He found himself listening for the clinking of mugs on his mother's tray.

A moment later she appeared at the door, looking from his father to himself with bright uncertain eyes.

'Here,' she said, 'have this. It will make you feel better.'

'To the future. To the future. To the future.'

He drank a little down before helping his gran with her bottle, and immediately the dead plant, the quarrel with his father, the strangeness of the girl on the bench seemed to dislodge themselves from his mind and dwindle in the light of a warm confident optimism.

But although he was quite sure that he had given his grandmother all of her Drink and that she had only dribbled the tiniest amount, she seemed unable to settle that night. Even after she had been put to bed and Paul's mother had come back into the lounge, quietly shutting the door behind her, they could hear the faint creak of the bed springs as she continued to rock herself forwards and backwards.

'She's really upset,' said his mother reproachfully. 'How could you go on at each other like that in front of her?'

In the middle of the night Paul woke to find the black rectangle of his bedroom door outlined in light. He could hear voices and cautious quick footsteps in the hall. He climbed out of bed feeling cold and confused. He opened his door. The hall was filled with light. The door to his grandmother's room was open, and leaning against the opposite wall staring in, he saw his father, wearing his nightclothes.

From the hidden room came a shrill lamenting and beseeching that seemed scarcely human. It could only be the rarely heard voice of the old lady, crying and fraily begging as if for her life, in a repeated monosyllable which might have been a word. 'See . . . See . . .'

'What is it?' he whispered. 'What's wrong with her?' He stood beside his father, staring into the room.

'She's upset, that's all. The doctor's with her.'

His mother knelt by the side of the bed, trying to soothe the old lady. A tall man stood beside her, holding the little glass feeding bottle to the light and measuring into it with great absorption a portion of golden liquid. The doctor. Still the frail distraught voice begged on and on. The word was quite articulate. 'Seed,' it sounded like. 'Seed.' But it held absolutely no meaning for them.

'If only I knew what it was I could get it for her,' said his mother helplessly. She was near to crying.

Deliberately the doctor adjusted the nipple of the feeding bottle and handed it down to her, saying gently, 'She'll take it better from you.' Then the voice subsided and they heard the familiar sound of the old lady's shallow eager sucking. In a few minutes they laid her back on the pillow, fast asleep.

'How old is she?' said the doctor quietly.

'Oh, ever so old. It says Pre-Enlightenment on her identity card. That's very old, isn't it? She's never been like this before, really. Never.'

'I've been through her records,' said the doctor, permitting himself for the first time to smile. 'She certainly has a clean bill of health. Quite senile over a long period. And beautifully cared for. You must be very proud of her.' He was a nice man to be so kind in the middle of the night. She smiled up at him and allowed him to see her anxiety.

'She is all right, doctor? You know. It's not the start of anything?'

'No, no,' he said. 'Nothing serious. Something they often pick up at this time of year. You'll be able to wheel her out soon. Take her down to the small enclosure by the shopping centre. They like it there. She'll pick up quickly enough. You'll see.'

'There's no danger?'

'No. None at all. We often come across these residual conditions. Even the most exhausted brain tosses them up from time to time. Odd words like this one. Archaisms.

But there's no real contamination from the past. It never develops into anything. Of course, we'll keep an eye on her, but you've nothing to fear.'

When the kind doctor had gone, giving Paul a brief and gloomy smile as he passed him in the corridor, Paul went back to his room and dialled his code number. He spelt out: QUERY: THE MEANING OF SEED, wondering if the spelling were correct. He still felt dazed and very tired, and looked stupidly at the blank screen for a few seconds before he grasped that the MEMORY was not working. He was frightened at first, remembering his misuse of it during the afternoon and the threat of disconnection. Then he realised that it was the middle of the night, a time when he had probably never had occasion to use it before. He climbed back into bed. As he fell asleep the artificial light shone dully through the curtain.

In the morning he woke and tried the MEMORY. It was working perfectly. He asked it the meaning of the word seed. It replied rather as the doctor had, that the word was an archaism, not relevant to modern society.

He switched it off and in the interval before his mother called him to breakfast he read and re-read the account of the fire, trying to imagine how it had been to be there as he knew he must have been. He held the little red feather up to his face and studied it intently, blew softly on it so that it stirred about on the palm of his hand, but no corresponding movement in his mind revealed its meaning.

He read and re-read the name Mrs Willmay. He repeated it in a whisper, but nothing yielded. Who she might be or what, if anything, she might have been to him was totally lost.

CHAPTER ELEVEN

THE FOLLOWING AFTERNOON, in bright sunlight robbed of all warmth by a sharp spring wind, Paul climbed to the top of Santan's Hill. He took his usual route down to the shopping centre and walked through the crowded promenade. Then, even though the plant was dead, he pushed through the swing doors into the bare courtyard that faced the small enclosure.

Sharon sat on the bench, turned sideways as if she only half watched for him. A gust of wind snatched strands of her hair and blew them across her face. Discarded plastic bags scurried against the base of the blank walls. Ahead of him, the thin upright twigs of the tree still visible through the blur of small leaves swung stiffly above the rigid bars of the fence. Everything that was free to move seemed restless and insubstantial in the wind.

He walked over to the bench and braced his arms on the back of it, staring at the tree.

After a moment Sharon said again, 'I'm ever so sorry about your plant, really I am.'

'It's not your fault.' She did not move. He wondered if he might just walk away, but he was held where he was by something unfinished between them.

After a moment she said, 'You don't know me, do you?'

'Yes. Sharon. Of course I do.'

'Who am I then?'

'You live in the hostel. You work up there somewhere. You come here. Every day.' He could not remember a day when she had not come.

'Do you know any more than that?' She spoke so earnestly.

'No. I'm sorry. I don't.'

She hesitated, looking about her. Then she spoke very quietly. 'A little while ago? A Mrs Willmay?'

Mrs Willmay. The name written in ink on the paper. He moved slowly around the bench and sat down beside her. 'Did you know her?'

'She is my mother.'

'That's so strange.'

'But you knew her name.'

'I have it written down on a piece of paper.'

'Let me see.'

He stood up to reach through his pocket into his jacket

lining and drew out the worn bits of paper. He sat down closer to her and unfolded them carefully so that the feather should not blow away.

'What's that?' she said, staring at it.

'I don't know. It's a feather. But I don't know why I have it. It brings me luck.'

She was frowning, digging in her own pocket. She pulled out an envelope, pinched it into a funnel and, reaching over, shook out onto the paper a second red feather exactly like his own.

'How did you get that?'

'Someone gave it to me. How did you get yours?'

'I don't know,' he said. 'I didn't write it down. I thought maybe you'd know.'

'I don't know either,' she said. 'I wasn't there at the time.'

He had begun to feel frightened. It seemed that at any moment she might reach behind her back and present him with something he did not want.

'You kissed me. Do you –' she paused – 'remember that?'

'No.' He shook his hanging head. 'No. I'm sorry. I only remember you here, on the bench, for a day or two, maybe more.' He was trembling. They had exchanged without looking at each other that contaminated word.

'You didn't write it down then, when you kissed me?'

'No.'

'Shall I forgive you, then?'

'If you want.' But he only felt for her fear and distaste. She could remember. Her mind was full of unthinkable things. He would have shifted away from her on the bench had she not looked so desolate that he pitied her. They sat in silence a moment before he said, 'You can remember, can't you?'

'Yes.' When he made no response, 'Everything. Back to when I was little. Before that, really. Things my mum told me about when she was little. Things her mum told her.'

'She could remember too?'

'That's why they took her away.'

'Are you ill too then?'

'No,' she said. 'There's nothing wrong with me. I did it on purpose.'

'But how?'

'I expect you know really. I did.'

After a moment, he said, 'It's the Drink, isn't it?'

'Yes. If you don't take it for three days you can remember.'

'Is that all?' he said.

'That's all.'

He felt less frightened of her now, but awed. His mind worked sluggishly, reaching out at what she might know, but trapped in its eternal box of three days' capacity. He remembered the dead plant, the girl who came to sit on the bench, the quarrel with his father, his grandmother's strange lament in the night. He said, 'Do you know what seeds are?'

'They're what plants grow out of.'

He tried to imagine a seed, but could only visualise a smaller and smaller plant.

'What about the feather. Who gave it to you?'

'My little brother.'

'Did I know him?'

'You must have seen him a couple of times. He's in a Home since Mum went. Up the Ackroyden. He had it. I found it on him the first time I went to see him in the Home. He said he found it out playing. He cried when I took it off him.' She began to cry too, so controlledly that it hardly altered the quality of her voice. But tears shone on her smooth cheeks, turned not towards him in any bid for sympathy but up to the sun. 'He said it brought him luck too. I thought it might get him into trouble, having it. It's off Mum's old parrot, isn't it?'

'I don't know where it comes from.' He was watching her caught in the meshes of memory, crying in sympathy with the tears of a child, who had long since stopped crying and played all unconcerned in some carpeted centrally heated Home quite ignorant of her existence. 'Why do you want to remember?' he said. 'Nobody makes us drink the Drink. We drink it because we like to. Because families love each other.'

She turned towards him, her face twisted out of shape,

her lips stretched harshly above her teeth. 'If I drank it I wouldn't love my mother, would I, because I bleeding well wouldn't know she existed.'

'Nothing lost matters,' he said, wanting only to comfort her.

'It's a lie!' she said. 'It's a lie. They only tell you that. She matters, doesn't she? Because as long as I remember her, who's to say she's lost? They pretend she doesn't exist and it's easy to get away with because they think no one still knows she exists. They think no one will ever find her, because no one will ever know to look for her. But I'll find her.' She went on staring at him after she had finished, breathing rapidly. After a while she said, 'You just don't want to know, do you?'

'There's no point for me.'

'Then why do you carry those old papers about?'

'I don't know. There's no point really.'

'You're in trouble, aren't you?'

'Not especially.'

'Why aren't you in school then? You've done something.'

'Yes. I suppose I have.'

'It's on that paper, isn't it? What does it say?'

'I don't understand what it says. I can't remember it at all.'

'Read it then.'

'It doesn't make sense really.' He unfolded the paper and read to her. 'I watched the dark area. I thought, what

144

holds it in? What if it spreads? At that moment there seemed to be an explosion of darkness, as if the dark were a source of energy so powerful that nothing could control it. I knew I must do something to stop the dark spreading. The lights came on again, but the dark had been sufficiently powerful to wipe them out. It was necessary to do something. When I passed the sports pavilion, I knew what I must do. There were cans of petrol in the storeroom for the team van, and boxes of matches . . .'

'Oh, Paul, was it you?' she said, smiling, laughing, who had shown till that moment no happiness in her. She moved suddenly forward and planted on his lips the long-forgotten kiss he had given her, scarcely loving, a hard little kiss of initiation. She frightened him again, but he could not afford to lose her.

'What does it mean? What's it about?'

'Last autumn someone burnt down the sports pavilion. Whoever would have thought it was you?'

'I suppose it must have been.'

'Maybe they'll send you away.'

'They don't seem to have done.'

'I'll remember you if they do.' She smiled, but she stood up. She was going away.

'Thanks,' he said. He wanted to ask her if she would come again, but he didn't. He got up, too, and stood by the high railings, sliding his hands up and down them as if they were the bars of his cage. It seemed to him suddenly that he had not understood the nature of the enclosure. It was not the trees that were enclosed. It was the Estate. Beyond the fence the narrow band of wild trees gestured and beckoned. He thought: *the fence protects us, the trees threaten us.* But the thought did not seem his. His mind felt under assault. He did not want to remember, but something like memory seemed to batter for entry.

He turned back to her and said harshly, 'I'll give up the Drink. I mean it.' Even as he said it and meant it, he thought with hopelessness of his mother's loving vigilance as she passed around the tray.

'There's no point for you.'

'I want to.'

'You don't know,' she said. 'You just say that.'

'I do know. I want to.'

'Go ahead then,' she said.

He could see she didn't believe him. 'I shall.'

'Goodbye,' she said.

'I shall,' he called after her, but almost immediately he turned back to the fence. It was made of metal, and still, where the sun had warmed it, smelt slightly of paint. Above the top cross lateral the spikes had been hammered out into flat-pointed triangles. When he stood on the concrete plinth into which they were sunk, he could just see over onto the grass.

He noticed then that a long twig had broken off at the foot of the nearest tree. No one had found it. No one had tidied it away. He wondered by law who it belonged to. Already he had twisted his big hand between the close protecting bars into the outer territory. He wanted it and closed his hand on it, dragging it back to the safe side of the fence.

He squatted down with his prize in his hand, looking at it avidly. At intervals along it were eruptions of new growth. He rubbed out one after the other with his thumbnail until they disappeared. Then, with his nail which was already moist and green, he began to scrape away at the rough skin of the twig, pulling it here and there with his fingers until the pale smooth core was revealed. He worked away at this for some minutes, stopping often to run it, smooth and hard, between his fingers, sniffing at the live green smell clinging to his hands.

When it was peeled quite bare, he began to walk along the inside of the fence, holding out his stick so that it rattled along the railings. The faster he walked the more light and musical became the rattle. When he reached the football pitches he began to run into the cold wind. The sound of the stick rose and sang.

A few uncaged trees still grew here at random along the fence. One so wild and untended that it reached right over the fence into the Estate. The branches, held upright like bunched fingers from a wrist, swayed woodenly in the wind. A half-metre from their tips, little baubles swung and tossed, a part of the tree. They glowed red-brown in the thick spring sun. Over the fence the nearest branch penetrated the aura of the Estate, so that he lashed at it with his stick, beating repeatedly at the invading twigs and the dancing balls until one of these detached itself and fell onto the pavement a little way in front of his feet. A gust of wind sent it bowling along the concrete ahead of him. On the shadowed pavement it looked black. He ran after it, reaching for it with the stick.

It had broken in falling, and as it hurtled away from him, bright yellow fluff began to burst from it in innumerable little explosions and shoot into the air like yellow smoke, rising with such vigour and determination that he was reminded of his descriptions of the fire. He remembered the words on the paper, *an explosion of darkness*. All around him now, yellow specks, in number out of all proportion to the size of the black case that had imprisoned them, spun upwards, exploded in sunlight. But for what purpose? For what possible purpose?

He began to run again, rattling his stick against the railings. The light had seemed to encircle the little patch of dark, but suddenly it had spread and drowned the light. The tiny black ball had broken and had revealed that it was far greater on the inside than on the outside. '*The inside is greater than the outside*,' sang the stick in the railings. '*The inside is greater than the outside*.'

CHAPTER TWELVE

THE TREES HAD seemed defenceless, caged for their safety in the small enclosure, ringed in by the Estate, the observation terraces, the confused, longing old ladies, and now, as if in a vision, he felt the Estate hemmed in, in its turn, by a world inhabited by trees.

Ahead of him, thickened and swollen by the spring, another tree reached into the Estate. He ran at it, stick raised to beat it back, but something was in his way. He was jostled by boys smaller than he, boys out of school, some quite little boys, some as tall as he, leaping beside him, tearing at the tree, breaking off twigs that left white scars edged with green like blood starting to a wound.

They did not peel them carefully as he had done – there was no time now – only broke off smaller growths as they ran, sometimes ahead of Paul, sometimes at his heels. They didn't speak, but the noise of their shoes on the pavement and the ring of their sticks in the fence sent up a sound that deafened him. The railing came to an end embedded in the side of a building. The boy ahead of him hesitated and looked back, but Paul had already turned up a side road to his left and begun to jog along it, turning his head from side to side as if to pick up an old scent.

He did not keep to the pavement now, but ran along a long diagonal in the road. At the end of it he saw a woman pushing an old lady in a chair decked out with a bright spring blanket, hurrying home before the sun failed. She had already eased the chair down the ramp cut into the curbstone and started across the street, across Paul's path. He hesitated. He wanted to swerve, but he followed a line more powerful than himself. The side of the trolley struck him a glancing blow on the hip as he ran past. He heard the shrill frightened bleating of the old lady, the repeated screams of the woman. He heard the feet of the other boys pounding behind him.

Ahead of him, a block of flats rose like a cliff. At the base, facing him, were six identical blue doors. He hurled himself against the third door and began to lash furiously at it with his stick. After a moment he heard a chain rattle and a man's voice repeat in agitation, 'What is it? What is it? What's the matter?'

'Open it!' he shouted. 'Open it!' He never saw the man. He swung the door violently back onto him and began to blunder about the dark cramped passageway striking about him with his stick. Behind him he heard glass shatter and the stumbling of the other boys as they forced a way through the door.

He broke through a closed door into a room. Daylight shone through a red curtain giving the room a dull and angry look. He hated the room which should not have been there. He struck about him with his stick wanting to destroy it, but there was no time. Briefly, he saw a woman's face, mouth opened in a great silent scream that she was too frightened to release. He was tearing at a curtain, not pulling it sideways – there was no time for that – but wrenching it down off the rail.

'Stop!' shouted the woman's voice frantically. 'Stop doing that. What are you doing? Who are you?'

There was a heavy thud as some piece of furniture overturned and glass shattered again, this time under his foot as he kicked violently at the glass door that would release him.

He was in a bare brick courtyard which gave onto another street through a gate. He ran at the gate with his foot extended and kicked it off its catch so that it crashed against the outside wall and flung back at him with a retort like a gun. As if from a long distance he heard the woman's voice repeating, 'You didn't ought to have done that, you know. You didn't ought to have done that.' He heard the thudding and panting of the boys behind him. He was in a street again, a grey brick wall enclosed the delivery bay of the supermarket, empty of vans at this time of day, but with a squalid residue of plastic bags and the broken leaves of dead plants which he crushed underfoot as he ran.

And now there was no door where they must go, only a blank wall which he beat on frantically with his stick until it gave way and he was inside. The next wall of cardboard cartons was weightless and tumbled under his stick. He kicked them away with his feet.

The placid shoppers wheeled their trolleys in sudden panic out of the aisle he followed, but then there was a stand of tins in his way, blocking the line that must be kept free and all around him the boys were lashing it with their sticks. The tins with their ranks of photographs of dead plants collapsed, and bounced and rolled in the aisle. He seized one in his hand and flung it through the mirror which had doubled the ranks of dead plants stacked and sloped on green fringed paper. He crushed tomatoes under his feet as he ran, terrified by the noise and the confinement. For some time now the alarm bells had been ringing.

He was in the street again, running free. Confronting him was a wall higher than his head. It filled him with anger that it was there where it should not be. He attacked it with his stick, but the stick only jarred in his hand. He hurled himself against it, bruising his shoulder, but it did not crumble as it should have done. He gripped the stick between his teeth and leapt at the wall, grasping the top bricks with his hands and heaving himself up, struggling against the downward force of his own weight, kneeing the wall, scrabbling at it with the toes of his boots until he was lying on his stomach across it and could swing himself up by his arms into a sitting position.

Below, the other boys leapt and clamoured, their hair wild, their faces dirty and sweating. Two of the taller boys struggled up beside him. He straddled the wall and, gripping it with his knees, he reached down, caught a third by his jacket collar and hauled him up. The little boys were pushed up from below and lowered down the far side. Paul was the last to drop down from the wall, but they all waited for him. It was as if they were his friends and he their leader. He knew the line they must follow.

He ran on. He was ahead of the others now. He looked back once and saw them jogging in a troop some way from him. Ahead of him were the blocks of substandard housing. His hands were smarting from the wall. He changed his wand from hand to hand so that he might blow on and soothe the other. In the distance a siren wailed.

The roar of the motorway grew louder and louder. Ahead of him rose the boundary wall, but the line ran across it. It must be climbed. He ran across the uneven ground at the back of the substandards. The high grey wall tilted closer. Only the sky showed above it. It must be climbed. The voice of the motorway was articulated into the sound of individual vehicles – a hiss of air and tyres, constantly overlapping, but each reaching a blurred crescendo of sound, and fading. Beyond the wall would be a steep slope, a low wire fence, the slope steeper still, sheer onto the broad roadway which, too, must be crossed. How, did not yet occupy his mind, simply that he must cross it.

Although his hands had hurt him before, he hardly felt the scrape and jar of their bare contact with the wall. He was not aware, this time, of any difficulty in surmounting it. Below, the current of traffic surged steadily towards the central Estate. He did not stop to look at it, nor, this time, to wait for the others, who must fend for themselves. He lowered himself down the far side of the wall, the length of his arms, and dropped down onto the ground below.

Beyond the shelter of the wall, the roar of traffic bewildered him. Light flared off the shining roofs of the cars as they hurtled past. He had a confused impression that he might leap across them from one flashing surface to the next. The smell of petrol excited him. He began to run down the steep bank towards it, but almost immediately his feet slipped from under him. He was sliding uncontrollably towards the wire mesh fence, where now he saw for the first time, loosely strung out along the line of the fence, their plastic visors down, the Guardians lined up to intercept him.

CHAPTER THIRTEEN

PAUL WOKE AWARE of no disaster, only of smooth deliverance from a long and peaceful sleep. He lay with his eyes shut and a sensation of floating. At the very back of his mind it seemed that gleaming scales of different colours flashed light from the surface of a steady stream. The whole effect was very pleasing.

When, a moment later, he felt pain in his hands, which he seemed unable to move, and in one of his shoulders, that, too, seemed softened and kept at a distance. That he was not at home in his own bed never occurred to him.

Then he heard an alien sound. A chinking, ringing, growing louder as it moved towards him. He opened his eyes and did not know where he was. He shut them again, imagining that he had not woken at all, but fallen deeper back into sleep. There was, too, a smell of sterility. He opened them again. He was in a tiny room, painted pale green. A green cotton cover lay on the bed. It must be his own feet that made hillocks of green at the farther end. A green-painted door was set in the wall, less than a metre away from the foot of the bed, through which he prayed now that the rattling thing would not menace him.

It had reached the far side of the door. It stopped. The door was opened roughly, and a woman tightly fitted into a green nurse's uniform backed into the room, dragging after her a trolley. On it, covered metal basins and glass bottles clinked and shivered together. She manoeuvred it in the narrow space at the end of the bed and spoke to him with an unyielding cheerfulness.

'Well now, you must get ready.' It was as if she had caught him loitering. 'We must have you pretty for the psychiatrist. He'll be here in a minute, you know. Can you sit up?'

When he tried he could not. The white turnover of the sheet was tucked across his chest with such severity that it might have been a rope. His helpless hands lay on top of it, heavily bandaged, white on white, only the fingertips showing.

'Which is the bad shoulder, then?'

When he nodded towards the pain, which was close now and real, she hooked her hard arm under the other one and hauled him upright. With the other hand she piled pillows behind him. She sponged his face with a warm flannel produced from one of the basins and then battered at his hair with a brush that smelt of disinfectant. 'You look a treat.' She cocked her head to one side admiring not him, but her own handiwork.

'Is there a mirror?' he said.

'No. We don't keep them here.' Already she was backing out of the door dragging the trolley after her.

'Where am I?' But she had shut the door. Perhaps she could not hear.

Immediately the trolley had rattled away he heard footsteps outside the door. It opened very gently this time, almost cautiously. A man's face edged around it, lugubrious, sallow, heavily pouched under the eyes, and there eased in behind it a tall thin body in a brown suit. 'May I come in a moment and have a word with you?'

Although his voice and his bearing were so unassuming, this was no question. Without any pretence of waiting for an answer, the man was in the room, folding himself on the wooden chair against the wall, winding his long legs behind him, hooking his feet into the rungs. There he perched, his hands clasped on his pinched knees, closely regarding Paul.

'I'm Dr Palmer,' he said.

'Good morning, Father.'

'We've reached the afternoon, my son. How are you feeling now?'

'Quite well, thank you.'

'It's a beautiful day,' said Dr Palmer. 'The spring was very late, but finally it has come. I suppose you are unaware of that.'

Paul kept silent. The tiny room, the pain, the strange intruders left him feeling calm and clean and meek.

'I suppose the last day you remember would be a rather cold bright day, windy, with the coming of spring apparent, it seems, only to you and a few others. That was the day before yesterday.'

Paul said nothing.

The psychiatrist leant a little forward and said, 'What do you remember about that day?'

'Nothing,' said Paul.

'Oh come, give yourself a chance. Only forty-eight hours have passed. Lean back and shut your eyes. You'll find, I think, that it comes to you.'

'I don't want it to come.'

'Ah,' said Dr Palmer gently and sadly, 'but it must.'

'Where am I, Father?'

'You are in a hospital.'

'Why?'

'You must tell me that. You must remember.'

'Why do you use that word?'

'Because I think you'll realise in a minute that everything is open between us now. We can use any word that has meaning for us both. Tell me what you remember.'

He had been leaning towards Paul, sad gentle eyes and

voice directed upon him. Now he tipped back his chair against the wall, folded his arms behind his head and stared up at the ceiling as if he were prepared to wait indefinitely.

Paul, too, leaned back on the pillows. He felt suddenly very tired. The sense of well-being with which he had wakened seemed to have drained out of him. He shut his eyes as he had been told, and immediately his mind held the image of a woman standing in front of a red curtain with her mouth stretched open in a scream. Then he ran in the streets again. There was a wall across his path. It shouldn't be there. He could not stop running, but it was there, closer and closer. He cried out. His bandaged hand flew up before his face, and pain broke out in his shoulder. And then another wall. The tiny room seemed to close in upon him. There seemed not enough air to breathe.

As if he understood at once and shared the memory, being at once inside Paul and apart from him, Dr Palmer stood up, and moving rapidly past the side of the bed, reached to open a window behind Paul's head. 'It's nearly over now,' he said gently. 'All you have to do is tell me what you remember.'

Paul said, 'I was running. I ran through a woman's house. I must have broken something. She was shouting at me.'

'What were you running away from?'

'Nothing. It wasn't like that. There was a reason.' He sat forward in the bed, staring at the door. 'What was I doing?'

'Try to remember what frightened you just now.'

'There was a wall. It shouldn't have been there. I knew it was there, but I kept running towards it. I could feel the pain before it struck me. I thought it would go away. I ran right into it.'

'And then?' persisted Dr Palmer.

Paul lay back again. There was air to breathe. Bright space around him. 'I remember running down a slope in the sun.'

'Were you frightened?'

'No, Father. There were no walls after that. I felt happy.'

Dr Palmer went back to his chair. Tilted back against the wall, waiting again.

'When can I go home?' said Paul.

'Oh, we'll have you out of here in a day or so,' said Dr Palmer, shedding a sad smile from his sad face. 'There's nothing really wrong.'

It occurred to Paul with a small twist of fear that his question had not entirely been answered. He dared not persist.

'There's more, isn't there?' said Dr Palmer.

'Yes.' The light flashing from the car roofs. The smell of petrol crept into his throat. Grass slipped underfoot. He was falling, sliding, the last fence coming closer and closer. There were Guardians with whom he had struggled to let him climb that last fence. 'What was I doing?' he said to Dr Palmer.

'You must tell me, my son.'

'I was running towards the cars.'

'And if we hadn't stopped you?'

'I should have been killed.'

'Did you not think of that at the time?'

'No.'

'There were others too.'

He said blankly, 'What made me do that, Father?'

'You really don't remember why?' Each time he spoke the word, anxiety tightened. 'You were in the grip of the past. Haunted, if you like.'

'Contaminated?'

'If you prefer, contaminated.'

'But I swear to you I can't remember. I didn't know what I was doing.'

'But I know exactly what you were doing. You were running along a path that existed a hundred years ago, before the New Enlightenment. It doesn't exist now, but it was so real to you that you could not believe in the bricks and mortar of your own Estate when you saw them with your own eyes. You would have run to your death under that stream of cars rather than accept the reality of the present. You would have enticed others to their deaths had I not saved you from your illusions.'

'You? You saved me? I don't remember you.'

'Aberrations like this occur very occasionally, but we are always on the lookout for any indication. When two sightings of abnormal behaviour were reported and plotted, I saw at once that they had occurred at two consecutive points on the boundary line of the old settlement that lay here before this Estate was built. In the spring, boys and grown men even, ran along the boundary line striking at things, striking at one another with sticks. The whole ceremony was tied up in primitive superstitions. It died out even before the Enlightenment dawned.'

'Why do you talk to me like this?'

'Because it's too late to talk to you in any other way. It's odd,' he said, leaning back against the wall, 'these final interviews have a certain melancholy pleasure. So seldom can one speak one's mind direct.'

'I can't remember,' Paul repeated desperately, gesturing towards the doctor with one bandaged hand.

'Perhaps not, but you are deeply susceptible to the past. This is not the first incident. I would not call it memory so much as a kind of primitive urge, a collective memory that still erupts from time to time, even after three generations of the Enlightenment. We expect a few minor outbreaks at this time of year. You were present at one the other night in your own family.'

'My Gran?'

'Yes. The same sort of thing.'

'It was you,' said Paul. 'You were the doctor that came in the night.'

'That's right.'

'But they said you were a psychiatrist. A child psychiatrist.'

'It's a family service,' said Dr Palmer, with a shrug.

'What will you do with her?'

'Her? Nothing,' he said. 'Nothing at all. She's quite harmless. Your mother looks after her superbly. But you, Paul? What are we to do with you?'

'I don't know.'

'You do see that for your own good it is necessary that you go away for a time, till all this has blown over?'

'But my mother . . .'

'Oh, there's no need to distress her. She knows nothing at all about this. I've told her you've been selected for a sixth form symposium on Futurism in the Central Estate. She thinks you're in hospital for a final intelligence screening and expects you to be gone for three days. That should do the trick. You'll see her before you go. You'll find she's quite delighted with the whole idea.'

'But that's cruel.'

'More cruel than the truth?'

'Where do I really go?'

'We're checking out a vacancy now.'

'But there's no reason to send me away. I can't remember. Truly I can't remember.'

'But you have tried,' said Dr Palmer. 'You have tried to rob the MEMORY of things you had no right to keep. Contaminated papers were found on you, and a feather off that murdered parrot. We gave you every chance. Perhaps it's fair to say you are not responsible for what you do, but everyone on the Estates is under the same pressures. Others hold out. You have led younger boys astray. You are a danger to the Enlightened society. You have caused thousands of pounds worth of damage to your Estate. You have shown disrespect to the MEMORY.'

'But it doesn't answer. It lies. It steals things out of people's minds.' He was shouting, but he no longer cared. 'We are taught to use it and to entrust everything to it for safekeeping. We imagine it gives everything back, but it doesn't. It does what it pleases with us. Things aren't lost because they don't matter. They're lost because the MEMORY wants them lost.'

'You poor deluded boy. You quite fail to understand. The MEMORY only takes away what is damaging for you to know. It protects you. It loves you. At this moment it grieves over you.'

How can that be? he thought. *It is a machine.* He was staring at Dr Palmer, trying to transfer that sad exhausted face onto the figure of the man who had passed him in the passage outside his grandmother's room, who had smiled, he remembered, the same tired gentle smile. He said, 'She wanted something. It was a word I didn't know. When you had gone, I asked the MEMORY what the word was.'

'And it didn't answer.'

'It wasn't working at all.'

'Well?'

'Why?'

'But you know why, Paul. It wasn't working because I wasn't there.'

'Why are you telling me this?' said Paul. 'I'm not meant to know.'

'It doesn't matter now.'

'Why not?'

'Because there is nothing more that I can do for you. You are being sent away.'

'Soon?'

'In a day or two. As soon as we can make arrangements at the other end.'

'For how long?'

He did not answer, leaving Paul, in the silent seconds that engulfed the cubicle, to realise that there was no answer; that the unknown span of his lifetime was the only measure of his exclusion.

CHAPTER FOURTEEN

THE BUS LEFT for the centre on the following evening. Paul's mother, convinced of the existence of the course on Futurism, insisted on coming to see him off. When they reached the platform where the bus waited, she was disappointed to find no one else there.

'You'd think the other parents would come,' she said reproachfully. 'You'd think they'd want to come.'

Nor were there lights inside the bus. The figures already sitting there were indistinct, mere pale discs of faces against which the lights of the terminus reflected. 'That's odd,' she said. 'You'd think they'd send a proper bus.'

'Do go,' Paul said to her. 'There's no point in waiting.'

'Yes.' She hugged him fiercely. 'Yes, of course.'

'Goodbye.' He shouldered his rucksack in which she had carefully packed three days change of clothing.

'Goodbye.' She was crying, overwhelmed at the thought of their brief separation. As soon as she let go of him she looked away and began searching in her handbag for a handkerchief.

He climbed quickly aboard the darkened bus. It was nearly full, but he was only aware of the other people as barriers to his finding a place to sit. He had to go right to the back of the bus to find a seat by the window. He looked out, hoping to find his mother gone, the parting over. But she was still there, smiling brightly, waving with the handkerchief in her hand. He waved back. The bandages were removed from his hands and the grazes all but healed. She would suspect nothing. The enormity of what was happening to them left him numb.

In the last minutes, her ignorance of the truth seemed a mockery rather than a kindness. Her pride, her joy at seeing him set out to where she supposed he was going, made his isolation total. He felt that he must exchange with her some word of the truth. He rose to his feet and began to clutch at the handle of the small sliding glass panel above the sealed window, trying to force it open between them, but at that very moment the driver swung into his seat and set the motor vibrating. A second later the bus lurched so that Paul almost lost his footing. He sat down and pressed his forehead against the cold glass. His mother stood there, smiling and waving. The bus swung abruptly out of the terminus, and in seconds he had lost her.

In the dark crowded interior there was a sound of muffled weeping. No one spoke. The lights did not come on. They passed smoothly through the well-lit streets. He stared hungrily. Each corner, each building that he recognised seemed a foothold, a branch to catch at in this mad descent. But nothing could halt his passage. Smoothly and steadily, the Estate was sucked away into the past. He rolled his head back on the headrest of the seat, unable to look.

Someone had taken the seat beside him; a girl with straight fair hair that shone dully in the reflected street light. He noticed that she seemed quite unmoved by what was happening. She sat staring composedly ahead of her down the aisle of the bus, almost as if she were eager to be wherever they were going. So that he wondered briefly whether she knew at all what was happening, whether they had told her some lie to spare her. He was too miserable to be curious. He lay back against the coach seat, staring out of the window.

Very quickly they reached the peripheral road and swung off it onto the brilliantly lit motorway. Here the bus stopped for a moment. Two Guardians climbed aboard and took their seats by the driver. When they were out on the motorway, one of them worked his way along the aisle of the bus handing out cards. Paul's informed him that he was number 114783 to be disembarked at Halt D.

He glanced across at the girl's, which she had poked

carelessly in a crack in the back of the seat facing her. Another number. Another halt. He looked quickly at her face, wondering whether he might speak to her, but she had drooped her head into the corner of the seat and fallen fast asleep.

He timed the hours in the bus by the luminous hands on his watch. He wondered if he would sleep like the girl beside him, and envied her. She did not stir once, but slept on like one who has come to the satisfying end to a long task and need have no fears at all of waking, while he sat, hour after hour, oppressed with sorrow at what he had done. It lay like a physical pressure on his lungs. It seemed to interfere with his breathing. In his ignorance he imagined he would always remember each drawn-out minute, lit with the same garish intensity as his mother's slight waving form had been in the bus terminus. He thought he would never be free of the sights and sensations of the motorway and the night world glimpsed through the haze of light at its edge. It seemed that more and more would crowd in permanently upon the sparse furniture of his mind, until surely it must burst.

On and on they drove through an endless landscape of Estates on which he had no claim. Block upon block of patched light penetrated the glare of the street lights, each speck of light representing a family with an identity. His own was lost. He tried to drug himself with staring at these long miles of other invisible lives. But again and again an image formed in his mind, clearer than what he could actually see, of his mother and father and great-great-grandmother grouped in the lounge, sipping at the warm delicious draught that would destroy him, toasting a future that would exclude him utterly. So that, in three days, his mother, opening the door of his room, would feel puzzled, even experience the slight sense of loss that he had sometimes felt on waking. She would switch on the voided MEMORY by the bed, listen a while to its empty crackling, switch it off again, and leave, shaking her head, wondering who it was that had been there and would presumably return.

His watch recorded that they had been travelling for three hours when the bus finally turned off the motorway. It slowed its pace as it left the exit roundabout and came down a steep ramp onto a minor road. In minutes they were in a totally new world. The road was unlit. The lights of the last Estate receded. The driver switched on powerful headlights which bored into this new element of darkness. The road swung and turned, plunged and rose. The headlights grabbed suddenly at objects by the roadside. Now they caught a wall and picked out every single brick, now they sent a bright streak of light snaking ahead along a curb that twisted downhill. The landscape seemed quite bare. Above, for the first time in his life, he saw the stars, bright and sharp, and later, a moon wiped clean and shiny by the absence of any human light. Then, here and there in the dark spaces of the road, he made out isolated pinpricks of light which he could not interpret, and suddenly behind them, huge shallow domes, gleaming with the same cold gleam as the moon and pricked out at their bases with spotlights. They were set together in a great cluster stretching over a wide area with little space between them.

There was a stir of interest in the bus. He could hear a murmur of question and answer, all too indistinct to grasp. He glanced quickly at the girl beside him, but she slept peacefully on. He turned back to the window. Minutes later the bus drew to a halt. One of the Guardians stood at the end of the aisle and called out, 'Halt A. Will the following disembark.' He read out a series of numbers. Dark shapes rose in the bus, shouldered their new identities and moved slowly towards the door. He could hear the fear in their voices. 'Where's my luggage? What's happened to my luggage?'

'You'll find it outside the bus.'

'Is there anyone to meet us?'

'Where do we go?' He knew they questioned only to delay the moment they must climb out into the dark.

'Come along,' the Guardian kept saying, 'come along. You'll be told what to do outside.'

Outside, by Paul's window, was a wooden bus shelter lit by a single naked bulb and a storm lamp hung against the wall on a hook. A young man stood under the lamp, frowning in the poor light over a sheet of instructions pinned onto a board. The second Guardian was handing out suitcases and tossing them roughly into the shelter. One by one the people were herded out. The Guardian jumped aboard. The bus lurched forward again. Looking back, the group of people seemed tiny, clustered tightly in the pale pool of light with their suitcases about their feet. Above them, covering the long hillside, the domes shone, and suddenly, at a drop in the road, disappeared. The darkness was pricked here and there by patches and points of light. Then more domes, glowing over a great expanse of slightly raised ground. Another halt. More people herded out into the darkness.

At the third stop, the girl beside him rose suddenly to her feet. 'Goodbye,' she said, smiling at him. She was the first to climb off. He watched her walk quickly to the shelter and find her case. She carried it over and stood by the man who was waiting for them. The others crowded in front of the bus, grumbling, protesting, and the Guardian hurried them impatiently on. This was Halt C. His would be next. As they moved off, the girl waved to him and smiled again. He smiled back and felt suddenly lightened by her lack of concern. She was gone. *But I shall remember her*, he thought, and felt pleased.

More darkness. The glow of more domes. Halt D. Like the girl, he was quickly on his feet making his way down the aisle of the bus, looking at no one.

'Your number?' said the Guardian. Paul showed the card in silence, not looking at him. He climbed down the steps. The air was warm and smelt deliciously sweet. Above him, the stars were bright and near. He moved automatically to the shelter, picking up his rucksack as he went.

'Your number?' said the man standing there.

He held up the card in silence.

'You must memorise your number.'

He didn't answer.

One by one, the others joined him – a group of five, three boys near enough his own age, a sullen unshaven man in his thirties, a woman rather older, who looked about her in terror of the darkness. It frightened him too. Outside the pale circle cast by the lantern, it was total – thicker than air, without measurable depth. Only the strange domes put an end to it. And these he watched fixedly, concentrating his mind on them, allowing no access to the darkness.

When the bus had driven off, its red lights vanishing suddenly, then reappearing far out of reach as it climbed a hill, the man took the lantern off its hook and, ordering them to carry their cases, began to lead them along the narrow road. They walked in silence, their footsteps ringing on the ground. Silence such as they had never before experienced pressed in on them as smothering as the dark.

The lantern showed up the bars of a gate by the side of the road. The man stopped, holding his lantern first to the number painted on it, then to his list. He read out a number. They fumbled for their cards and stretched them into the lantern light. One of the boys. The gate was opened and he was despatched down an invisible track at the end of which a naked lightbulb hung over what was just discernible as a door. No one said goodbye to him. He disappeared into the blackness.

At the next gate it was the woman's turn. She began to moan when the gate was opened for her. The man caught her by the arm and began to direct her towards it, but she broke violently from him and hurled herself back among the others, gripping at their arms, clinging to them with astonishing strength, sobbing with fear.

'Come on,' said their guide roughly. 'We haven't all night. Here,' he said to the older man, 'you take her down there. We'll wait.'

'No,' said the woman. 'No.'

'Come on,' the guide said. 'Or otherwise we'll leave you. No one else is going to take you in.' She went then, clinging to the man's arm, crying harshly. The others stood waiting in silence. A door opened. Its rectangular space filled with faint light, and a dark human shape. The woman was led in. The door closed. The man's feet could be heard crunching back up the path.

The diminished troop moved on again. At the next gate Paul's number was read out. He walked without a word down the path, feeling his way through the dark towards the door with its overhanging bulb that would admit him.

He did not look back at the retreating lantern. He could hear the footsteps fade on the road. Ahead of him, the door opened as if someone had watched for him. 'Come in,' said a man's voice.

The stranger stood in shadow, pressed against the wall of a narrow entrance, holding the door with one hand and extending in the other a lighted candle on a saucer. Immediately opposite the door a narrow staircase led steeply upwards. The man shut the door behind Paul and then, framed in candlelight, began to mount the noisy stairs. Paul followed. He had not clearly seen the man's face, but his voice as he said, 'You'll be tired and want to be in bed,' had seemed comfortable in its air of command. Paul had expected to fear, and found he did not.

The rest of the house was dark and silent. He could not guess at its size, but felt it heavy with the weight of sleeping people. The man showed him the bathroom and gave him the candle. When Paul came out, he was waiting in the darkened hall. He opened the door into a minute bedroom. 'That's yours,' he said. 'Keep the candle, but don't waste it. Goodnight,' he added.

'Goodnight,' said Paul.

He shut his door and a moment later heard another door shut a little way down the passage. He took his pyjamas from the top of the rucksack and changed by candlelight. For a moment he sat on the edge of the bed, staring at the flame, the tiny fire. Then he blew it out.

The sheets were rough and smelt of damp. The bed felt unfamiliar. It was his first night without the Drink. He wondered if it would be possible to sleep at all. He lay for a while with his eyes open in the dark. The images of the journey played before him. The strange luminous domes, the girl standing smiling at the wayside halt, the yellow glare of the motorway, back and back he travelled to the rhythm of the engine, until he saw his mother waving by the bus. Suddenly, overwhelmingly, he was tired, as the man with the candle had said he would be. He fell deeply asleep.

CHAPTER FIFTEEN

HE WAS AWAKENED by blinding light against which he tightened his eyes and pressed his face into the hard pillow, fighting for the illusion that he was in his own bed with the sunshine pouring through the window.

Before he would accept the truth he groped by his bed for the familiar knobs of the MEMORY, which would at a touch comfort the sense of loss, the sense of being lost, that took a transitory hold on waking. There was nothing there. His hand groped on the seat of a wooden chair drawn up by the bed and closed only on the identity card he had been given on the bus. An electric light bulb blazed in the ceiling of a bare little room. Nothing. No voice to tell him who he was. No voice to tell him what to do. He whispered the code number with which he had contacted the MEMORY and looked at the card in his hand. The two numbers bore no resemblance to each other. He thought, *I do not exist.*

His mother, his father, his gran, his home – the terms of his existence were gone. He thought, *I will remember them.* He remembered his mother standing in the bus station and felt only pain. *It will go away*, he thought. *The pain will go away.* But it made no move. It remained with the dwindling waving figure, held there however far the bus might travel, impossible to escape from, impossible to retrieve. Sleep had been a respite.

He swung his feet over the side of the bed and sat with his head clasped in his hands, trying to collect his thoughts. He could smell the warm familiar smell of porridge cooking. His clothes, he noticed, had been removed from the end of the bed, and others set in their place. He lifted them one by one and inspected them. Thick cord trousers, a checked shirt, thick socks, a pullover, a pair of boots on the floor. They had been washed and pressed and mended. They had been a part of someone else. Dressed in them, he would have surrendered more of himself. Nevertheless, he slowly put them on and found them only slightly small. Two lengths of string hung side by side over the end of the bed. He could think of no use for them, but clearly whoever had entered his room as he slept, had set them there with a purpose.

For he had been sent here with some purpose, which was quite beyond his imagining. He had a strange sense that somewhere beyond this door or beyond the next, a drama waited for him to enter and take up some role dictated by the strange clothes. He sat, dressed and ready, on the side of the bed, pulling the lengths of twine through his fingers, waiting to be told what to do.

Through the thin walls on either side of him, he heard the contaminated people come creaking from their beds, blundering in the small spaces as they dressed. On the floor below, a woman was singing, not one of the gentle aimless airs his mother sang, but a brisk repetitive chant that rose suddenly to a shriek of, 'Breakfast!' Heavy footsteps rattled on the bare stair boards. Then silence. He waited until he heard a door slam. Then he twisted the string around his hands, poked it into his pocket and came slowly onto the landing. The square outline of the window opposite was distinct with grey early light.

He went down the stairs putting his weight on the unsteady handrail, making as little noise as he could in his heavy boots. He thought of the people he had heard assembled in the room below. Listening for his approach, waiting for him to open the door and reveal himself. He wondered what they intended for him.

But when he stood in the cramped passageway which led from the foot of the stairs to the front door, the mutter of conversation behind the door on his right never ceased. Only when he opened it was there silence. There in the uncompromising electric light, five men were seated about a table. Their skin was very dark, their eyes, by contrast, light and wild, their teeth white between parted lips, their hair long and ill-kempt. They stared at him. Behind their eyes lurked their congested minds. He could feel their hostility.

Among them he recognised the man who had admitted him the night before. He had scarcely seen him then, but had imagined from his tone that he was in authority, a man of the Estates. Now he saw that he was merely another of the contaminated. He said quietly, 'Come on in and sit down, boy.' The others shifted together on the two forms which flanked the table and began again to talk amongst themselves, as if they assumed him unable to hear or speak.

'Who's this then?'

'New Lad, like I told you.'

'Boy, more likely. He's never a Lad.'

'What's his age then, Lord?'

'What's your age, Boy?'

'Sixteen,' said Paul.

'Sixteen,' he interpreted to the others.

'He's too young.'

'Straight from the Estates then, is he, Lord?'

'Last night.'

'How'll he manage, then? You're never going to put him on the contract.'

'No choice but to,' said the man they called Lord. 'He'll manage by having to.'

Paul noticed that he always spoke with the same quiet finality, as if he knew the rules of life so well and had accepted them so long, that everything he said must be the last word on the subject. Paul watched him, watched them all, with the same detachment with which they discussed him; neither he nor they able in any way to conceive of belonging to the same world inhabited by the other.

This man, Lord, to whom they all referred was slightly older than the rest. The brown creased surface of his skin seemed like a transparency through which the glowing blood shone. His eyes were small, close set to the bridge of a long nose. His hair rose from his head, stiff and wiry. Through it gleamed the taut brown skin across his skull, reflecting the light. Now, with a quick authoritative nod, he said, 'Have your breakfast, Boy.' He never smiled. 'Rake,' he called. 'More porridge.'

A woman came out from behind a partition wall carrying a steaming pan with both hands, gripping the handle. She came to the head of the table. She was dressed as all of them were, in corded trousers with a loose shirt made for a man, hanging out at the waist. Her dark hair was tied tightly back in a long straight tail. He noticed that she was very handsome, or had been, for to Paul she was as good as old. He wondered why she had come here. He was watching her and she, drawn to notice him, let the heavy pan down suddenly on the end of the table so that the spoons and bowls rattled. She stared eagerly at him.

'Paul,' she said. 'It is Paul, isn't it?' The men looked with silent curiosity from one to the other.

The sound of his name making it undeniable that it was he, called Paul, in this room with these people, unnerved him. He said more sharply than he intended, 'I don't know you.'

'You know him then?' Lord said to the woman.

She looked searchingly once more at Paul. Then, putting a ladleful of porridge into his bowl and smiling at him, she said quickly, 'Yes, well, I must have done somewhere or other, else I wouldn't have known his name, would I?'

When she was out of the room Lord said, 'Was your name Paul?'

'Yes.'

'Well, it's not now,' said one of the younger men. 'It's Boy now, same as I'm Hook and he's Lord. Same as he's Binder, and he's Lady. It's Boy, do you see, until you're raised to Lad.'

He looked from one to the other, trying to distinguish one wild dark face from the next. There was Lord. There was the young man, Hook, who had just spoken. There was a sour-faced man called Lady. Binder's face was round and kindly. There was the woman who had mistaken him for someone else. At that moment the light went out.

The men grunted and pushed back the forms. The grey window square brightened in the dark wall as his eyes recovered from the sudden loss of light. All around it he noticed now the shapes of plants growing in pots looking out to the light.

'Ready then?' asked Lord.

'Ready.' They were standing crowding towards the door. The woman, Rake, came in from the kitchen carrying plastic bagfuls of sandwiches on a tray. She came back with a bunch of small tin pails dangling from each hand. Each reached for his own. They grunted their thanks.

Paul, seeing when they rose that they all had tied string tightly around their trouser legs below the knees, retrieved the two lengths from his pocket and quickly did the same, out of an instinct to imitate them as closely as possible. Propping one boot after another on the form, he bound and tied the string.

All the time, the woman stood at a little distance, watching him, patiently holding his bag of sandwiches in one hand and his tin pail in the other. When he stood up she held them out to him.

'Here,' she said. 'Take your lunch. Don't let the others talk you out of any of it. You'll need your strength.' She spoke kindly. The others had left the room. She put her hand on his arm and turned him towards her, so that he faced her in the growing light from the window. Clean strong features, clear arched brows, grey flecked eyes.

'You don't know me, do you?'

'No,' he said. He was ashamed that he had answered her harshly before, but he did not know how to apologise.

'You will,' she said eagerly. 'In a day or two you will.'

'Who are you?'

'You wait,' she said, smiling at him. 'It won't mean a thing to you if I tell you now. Better it comes to you in its own good time. But you'll be pleased, I think,' she said shyly. 'I was a friend of yours in a way. You'll be glad of a friend here, and so shall I. Hurry now.' She gave his arm a little shake before relinquishing it. 'Lord's not patient with laggards. Don't forget your hat.'

In the hall a wide-brimmed straw hat hung by a row of empty pegs. He lifted it down and put it on. She followed him to the door and waved over his head. The knot of men by the gate, all hatted as he was, waved back as Paul ran up the path to join them.

They walked along in silence. The dawn was a fragile thing, not to be done any violence upon. The sun had hardly risen to confirm it. The day's breath played on his face, cool still, and very sweet to smell. They filed in order down a narrow lane passing little gardens of living food and orchards of uncaged trees, and one or two cottages like the one in which he had slept. No sign of life came from them.

'Who lives there?' he said to Hook.

'Weeders, Dibbers, Sowers. That sort,' said Hook with contempt.

'So what are you then?'

'Don't you know?'

'I'm asking.'

'Reapers, of course. You don't think I'd be seen dead with any of those others.'

There was silence again, the corrugations of their corduroys sang as they walked. The wire handles of their tin pails creaked. Their boots rang sharp on the stony ground.

'What do Reapers do?'

'Cut the bloody stuff,' said Hook. 'Dead ignorant, aren't you. But then you're off the Estates.'

Paul did not know how to answer that. No one had ever before suggested that he was ignorant. He wondered of what Hook's knowledge consisted. 'Do we have far to go?'

'Nah,' he said with the same crushing scorn.

The sleeping cottages were behind them. The path had begun to climb. Ahead lay one of the smooth hillsides he had seen from the coach, not now a black shape, but covered with smooth soft green from which the domes rose like giant clustered blisters, opalescent in the dew.

'Do we work in there?'

'What do y'think?' said Hook.

Apart from the domes there was nothing. No fence, no wall, only hillside and sky, as if one might be sucked through the gaps between the domes and on and on, with no man-made barrier to cling to. He shivered although the sun had risen now and reached him as they climbed.

At the crest of the hill the path was crossed by a wide track, worn and flattened, but they ignored this and moved forward. Their own path widened out and then gave onto a broad concrete road, leading directly to the first of the domes.

Ahead of them Paul saw two Guardians. They wore the same white uniforms as on the Estates, the same white bulbous helmets. He dared not ask the scornful Hook why they were there. First one, now two, apparently waiting for them. The party had moved along at a rapid steady pace; now, at a backward signal from Lord, they slowed to a dignified walk. He moved slightly ahead of the rest. A third Guardian joined the other two. They stood with their legs astride, barring the path, their thumbs hooked into the wide black belts from which their revolvers hung. The sun focused in a bright intense pool on each white helmet. Their lowered visors reflected the steady advance of the Reapers.

Lord reached behind his back again to signal the others to stop, and he himself moved forward a pace or two. The central of the three Guardians moved forward to meet him.

'Lord?' blared the microphone voice.

'That'll be me, sir.'

'What complement have you brought?'

'Self, three men and a half, three-quarters really, but he's straight off the Estates, and don't count as Lad till his strength's up.'

'Come with me, then.'

A small hut stood at a little distance from the dome's entrance. Beside it, Paul saw a large red wheel raised from the ground by a pipe, apparently part of some water system. Into this hut Lord and the head Guardian disappeared. The other two Guardians shifted together to block the path, and stood rigid and faceless behind their visors, their gloved hands straying on and off their swollen holsters, watching without seeming to see.

The tension of waiting tightened. Deformed as they were into solid eyeless blocks by their uniforms, Paul sensed the alertness of the Guardians. The Reapers stood together watching the hut with set brown faces as unrevealing as the darkened visors. They turned the brims of their hats in their hands. No one spoke.

Now, more Guardians appeared on an iron stairway leading down the side of a two storey concrete block attached to the side of the dome. Paul counted them jogging forward in a loose formation, one, two, three, four. They took up position with the others, lengthening the line across the path. The door of the hut opened. The Guardians shuffled to attention, shoulder to shoulder. Their leader appeared and marched briskly towards them, with Lord following respectfully a few paces behind. When he reached the path he called out a brief order. The rank of Guardians broke in two and smartly reformed, flanking the path. They had drawn their revolvers as they moved. They closed in at the rear as if to block escape.

Lord, with no more than a glance at his own men, strode between them, small, erect, fearless. The Reapers filed behind. Now the Guardians closed in and began to chant through their grating microphones, '*Left, right, left, right.*' They jogged in time to their own commands, so that the Reapers were forced to jog at the same unthinking pace, with the chorus of orders blaring in upon them. '*Left, right, left, right,*' dashing them forward against the metal doors of the dome.

By some remotely controlled mechanism, the iron bar flew up at their approach and the glittering doors swerved outward on semi-circular tracks. The din of the microphones intensified. In the confusion of sound Paul was swept through the doors.

Behind him he heard the metal doors shutting and the clank of the iron bar locking them in place. Ahead, the whole circumference enclosed by the dome was filled with upright plants – long stalks carrying heads, rich copper bronze in colour, standing stiff and still as if under some perpetual order of attention. For they were alive. The dry delicious smell that filled the stifling atmosphere of the dome could only come from something living. For a moment there was silence. Then, from a small observation window halfway up one side of the dome a microphone crackled hugely at the intake of a magnified breath, and a voice blared, 'I'll put it out to you.'

Lord cupped his hands to his mouth and shouted to the

roof of the dome, 'I'll take it.' Immediately, he clapped his hat back on his head.

The little band of Reapers followed suit. They stood at the edge of the field, looking upwards, and Paul, following their look, saw two glistening silver spheres, suspended at some distance apart between the irrigation pipes that latticed the shallow translucent dome. There was a vicious crackle as a naked electric current darted like lightning between the two spheres. It must be the signal for which they had waited. They moved, all as one, to a rack built close beside the door where there hung a row of curved gleaming knives. For killing. For killing the beautiful dry plants that stood waiting, motionless and indifferent.

Because the others each took a knife, Paul, who had raged against his father over the death of a single plant, took one too and, as they did, helped himself to an oblong stone and a pair of worn leather gloves that lay ranged neatly on the shelf below the knives. He pulled on the gloves, changing the stone and the knife from hand to hand, watching the others, waiting for the killing to begin.

They were slowly shuffling together, edging Paul with them, until they had formed a circle by the side of the standing corn. Heads bowed low so that the brims of their hats grated together, arms extended into the centre of the ring. He watched them sideways, doing what they did. They brought their arms slowly from their sides, the sickle in one, the whetstone in the other, extending them into the circle's centre.

'Now,' said Lord. He began to clatter the one against the other, stone against blade. Then each of them opened his mouth and sounded a great low note of lament. '*Oah! Oah! Oah!*' The men's deep voices ringing above the ringing sound of the tools.

Paul shook with terror at the sound. He struggled to make it too, but his throat was rigid. No sound escaped it. The low full note held as the Reapers raised their heads, and then as their arms stretched high to the roof of the dome, they flung back their heads and let out a last shrill cry, '*Ahhhhh.*' He had thought they cried out of grief, now this seemed a shout of wild release. Their arms and heads slumped, but Paul raised his at once and looked around in an agony of fear, lest after this shout of defiance the Guardians should be provoked into action against them. But there were no Guardians. He looked around him at the whole wide area of the dome, empty and silent except for the Reapers, who stood upright now, testing their blades on the palms of their hands, smiling at one another. No sign of a white helmet. They were quite alone.

'What do you think of it, Boy?' asked Lord.

He said, 'It's as if it all belonged to us.'

'Who else?' said Lord happily. 'Who else has it ever belonged to?'

They began to cut the corn at seven in the morning.

At noon they rested for an hour, walking back across the crunching stubble, between the stooks neatly trussed by Binder. They sat with their backs propped against the concrete foundation of the dome, eating sandwiches and drinking beer. Already Paul was exhausted.

'Will we do it, Lord?' asked Lady gloomily.

'Should do,' said Lord. All the time he munched his sandwiches, his eyes assessed the crown of standing corn inside the ring of stubble.

'We're behind.'

'We've got till seven.'

'We're behind, though.'

It was Paul's fault. It must be done by a certain time, and he was slowing them down, trailing way behind the line of Reapers, grip, bend, strike, till, looking up with the sweat stinging his eyes, he saw the line halt, watching him impatiently. Already his back and the backs of his legs and a band across his shoulders like a yoke, felt weak and heavy.

They broke again at four and drank cold tea from the tin pails. Paul saw them watching him anxiously. He was very tired. The new skin on the palms of his hands had blistered even through the thick gloves. His bruised shoulder ached. There was a dense substance inside his skull, expanding, bringing pressure against his eyeballs from behind so that they seemed to protrude and smart. He wanted to remain where he was with a grim leaden passion.

'He's done in,' said Binder. 'Can't you get him off?'

'He's on the contract.'

'Couldn't we hide him out there?'

'They'd see,' said Lord, glancing up at the observation window.

The shame of his weakness didn't touch him. He hated Lord. Nevertheless, when the others rose and stood looking down at him, not angrily but with concern, he managed to rise painfully to his feet and cross the widened band of stubble to the corn.

Again they formed the line behind Lord. Again they gripped and bent and struck. He lost all sense of what he was doing, simply acted out again and again a pattern of pain, breathing the dry dust of the dead plants into his sore shrinking lungs. He no longer looked up, but sensed dully that he was alone with his task, the others having far outstripped him.

Until he heard jeering voices close at hand. Then he raised his head and saw through blurred eyes, not the expanse of corn but a ring of brown faces. They had reached the centre. It was done but for a single handful of corn.

'Go on, Boy,' said Lord. He was laughing, his face distorted with mockery. 'It's all yours.'

'Get it then.'

'Get on with it!'

They were pointing their sickles at him, glaring oddly. Their eyes glittered white in their brown filthy faces. The deadening exhaustion was suddenly driven out of him by terror. He turned rapidly this way and that. The wild, vicious cries increased. He was surrounded by them. He could smell them everywhere. Gleams of light from their knife blades stabbed his eyes. There was no escaping them. No alternative. He knew what he must do, as with the fires, as with the bird, as with the wild running. He raised his knife. The cries rose all about him.

'*What havee? What havee? What havee?*'

He grasped, with sickening revulsion, the last of the living corn, whom he was, and killed it, although it was himself, with a loud harsh cry, which the stronger voices lifted and carried above his head.

'*A neck! A neck! A neck!*'

He saw their faces close in upon him. Felt their hands. Knew that they bound him, carefully, in straw – arms and legs. It scratched against his face, caught in his hair. They replaced his hat. They spoke gently now. He felt them lift him and carry him. His eyes were open. He saw the cloud-like dome. He saw the spheres gleaming among the narrow lattice of pipes. He heard the whirr of the doors, the weak mechanical voices of the Guardians. And then he was still being carried, face upwards, staring up into a space of deep blue. Light had faded from the sky, but not before the harvest had been taken, the contract kept.

CHAPTER SIXTEEN

HE WOKE IN the bed in the cottage. His tired body lay weighted to the hard mattress, but his mind rested light and relieved. Before the harvest, he had been cut adrift in space and apprehension. Now it seemed that he was cast up on some still shore out of reach of all that he had dreaded. He remembered his terror and its release, the gentle hands binding him in sweet-smelling straw, the kind voices.

The window was bright with sunlight. He slept and woke again, and found the light on the walls altered. He sat up stiffly and, dragging his clothes onto the bed beside him, began slowly and painfully to dress. He could hear no sound in the house. He wondered if he were alone in it. He was very hungry.

He went downstairs and opened the door of the kitchen. Light blazed at the window and cut obliquely across the floor from the open doorway. Outside, he heard men's voices and the flat ring of hoes, but the dark cluttered segments of the room were quiet and contained.

The woman called Rake sat near the garden door, sewing. She looked up at him as he came in, shifting her spectacles up on her nose and smiling. 'You've slept well,' she said.

'Is it very late?'

'Two-ish. Don't worry. There's always a day off after a harvest. Sit down. You must be hungry.' She pointed to the table and, rising herself, folded away her mending.

Paul slid onto the farside bench and watched her cross back and forth across the shaft of thick, dusty sunlight, lifting a plate from a rack, moving behind the kitchen partition to take a covered dish from the oven. She moved impulsively, breaking off as she passed the window to finger the soil in the plant pots and sniff at the leaves. A bird in a cage had been hung in the sunshine from a hook over the door. She stopped, with the steaming plate of vegetables in her hand, to whistle at it. Then she came towards the table with the sunlight behind her firing the edges of her hair, darkening her face.

Paul stood. The bench behind his knees scraped back. He held out his hand to her shyly. 'You're Ellie Willmay, aren't you?'

'You've remembered.'

'Yes.'

She set the plate abruptly down on the table and ignoring his hand, gripped his two arms above the elbow, holding him at a little distance as if she would have embraced him but needed, too, to watch his face. The tears on her cheeks shone on her faded skin. 'The children,' she said. 'Where are the children?'

'Sharon's here.'

'Sharon, here? What do you mean, here?'

'At the Halt before this. She was on the bus, sitting beside me, only I didn't know her then. Just now when I saw you, I remembered.'

She took a handkerchief from her sleeve and, pushing up her spectacles, rubbed harshly at her eyes. 'Oh, whatever is she doing here? What's she gone and done now? She was meant to stay with the little ones.'

'They're all right,' he said. 'They're all right. They're in a Home. They're happy. She went to see them.'

'She's not going to see them now. Getting herself sent down here. What does she mean by it?'

He said gently, 'They didn't know her when she went. They were quite happy.'

Ellie folded her arms on the table and burying her head in them gave way to weeping. Then she wiped her eyes again, and reaching out her hand said eagerly, 'You're sure it was her?'

'Yes. She was the same. I'd only seen her a day or two before.' He smiled at her. 'It's you that's different.'

She laughed, with her face still wet. 'I was fat, wasn't I? How'd you ever know me, Paul?'

'From the photograph. And you knowing me. I didn't know many people.' He had begun to eat, and spoke between mouthfuls of potatoes.

'Queer sort of life, wasn't it?' said Ellie.

'Better than this.'

'No,' she said. 'No. For you, especially. I had the kids, but it was no sort of a life for a boy. You're tired now, but once you've got your strength you'll see it differently. You'll be glad you're here. It's a good life. Anyway, there's no going back.' She threw back her head and laughed. 'What I wouldn't give for a ciggy now. Right this minute. And Sharon,' she said, with tears in her eyes again. 'Fancy, Sharon. We'll see her then, sooner or later. I never thought to see any of them ever again.'

But two months passed before the Reapers were sent to the domes to the East of their own settlement. During that time they were kept constantly busy, harvesting in succession crops that kept to their own intricately staggered seasons within their separate domes. So that the Reapers, emerging with their straw man from a completed contract, parched with dust and stained with sweat, might meet the Sowers issuing from the very next dome with their hats over their ears, their rough sacking cloaks glistening with moisture clasped about their shoulders to protect them against the chill play of spring rain from the irrigation system, which even now a Guardian was adjusting by the watercock near the entrance.

They would pass each other with nods or short grunted greetings, for the Reapers had little to do with the Sowers. They despised them for the closeness of their contact with the soil. The Reapers were very proud, a caste apart. They kept in closest contact with the particular band of Weeders that preceded them from dome to dome – simple people, even less skilled than the Sowers, but friendly, given to gossip and therefore useful sources of information.

One evening, towards the end of June, the Reapers were enjoying the late sun in their garden. They had finished a contract the night before and had spent the day bathing and sleeping in. Only in the last hour had they summoned the energy to work in their vegetable patches.

Paul sat with his shoulders against the warm brick wall of the cottage. Bees racketed in the honeysuckle over his head. He breathed in long breaths of the heavy scent of warmed nectar. Sun blazed beyond the shining fringes of his eyes. He could feel it on his face and on his arms; feel it working on the back of his hand and on the flagstone on which it lay to make them both one substance. The sun had transformed him. His face and arms were baked brown. His hair, which started from his head uncut and untended, was bleached to a fine gold. Constant harvesting had strengthened him quickly. Twice now he had not been forced to cut the neck and carried from the field; he had beaten Hook once, and at the last harvest, both Hook and Binder.

He was no longer Boy but Lad. He sat with the warmed bricks pressed against his shoulder blades, feeling entirely happy. He could not believe there was winter in this place. The sun had absorbed him.

It was sinking now behind a row of trees that could not contain it in their broad flat leaves. Light flared out, shot shafts, consumed whole branches in flame until at last the sun was truly netted and dragged down below the hedge at the end of their garden, just as their friends the Weeders filed along the path beyond it with their forked sticks held on their shoulders.

'You been up the Eastern domes yet?' Lord called out to them. Paul got to his feet and joined him by the hedge.

'Just started today,' said the Weeder.

'How's the corn?'

'There'll be one ripe for you by next week. Wouldn't you say, Groundsel?' (For having all the same lowly task and no hope of promotion, they were called after their victims.)

'Next week or the one after.'

'A Midsummer harvest?'

'Thereabouts.'

'Ask about, would you?' said Paul. 'See if there's anything about a new girl moving into one of the cottages there.'

'Thinking of going courting then?' asked the Weeder,

much amused. 'You'd better watch it. The Lord will be down for Midsummer. He'll have his eye on you.'

'What Lord?' said Paul when he was gone. 'You're Lord.'

'Harvest Lord. There's a real Lord who owns it all.'

'I'd supposed the Estate owned it.'

'Well, they let him run it. It's his domain you might say. He works this lot of domes and those to the East as experimental stations. Perfecting the crops and such. All on convict labour. He can't go wrong really. Makes a fortune out of it, they say. Not that he's here much. Christmas, some years, for a day or two, and always for a week at Midsummer.'

'What does he do?'

'Walks about in fancy dress. All posh and pale as a lily,' said Binder with a laugh. 'Looks in charge. Plays God to the Guardians.'

'Keeps a wide berth of the harvest field,' said Lady grimly, battering the earth with his hoe. Paul could feel them gathering together in their dislike of this man. He wanted to be among them.

'And us?'

'Oh, he takes an interest in us all right,' said Hook with scorn. 'We're his good little children, see? Remembers us all by name. Knows everything about us.'

'How can he, if he's off the Estates – remember from Christmas to Midsummer?'

Their laughter had a ring of bitterness. 'You'll know when you see him, Lad,' said Lord. 'You wait.'

The following evening the same Weeder looked over the hedge on his way from work and reported that a new girl had turned up there towards the end of April. Pretty little thing, by all accounts. They'd given her a job at the Home for Recalcitrant Old Ladies, which the Weeder's informant had thought a waste for one of such obvious talent.

A week later, when the latest crop had been harvested from the nearby domes, Lord had time to walk over to the Eastern settlement to put in a bid for the ripe crop mentioned by the Weeder. It would be a long walk there and back, taking up the best part of the day, and there was only the Weeder's word for it that the contract had not been given out to a more local team. However, he thought the journey worth the risk, especially as it would provide Ellie with a chance to search for her daughter. She asked if Paul might come too, and Lord agreed.

They set out after breakfast, climbing the path to the domes and then turning left along the wide worn track that Paul had noticed on the morning of his first harvest. They followed this eastwards, seeing ahead of them nothing but sky and the smooth undulations of this bare land. Although it was Midsummer, the real weather had been very dry, and on this thin soil the wild grasses had dried and bleached. The stony track lay like a wide faded ribbon folded over the shapes of the downs. The hedges that flanked it were pale with dust.

Towards noon they climbed a slight rise and could see both the domes they had left and the domes ahead of them, swollen and white against the pale browns of the sparse landscape.

'If you kept going along it, would you come to the Estates again?' Paul asked Ellie. They had stopped to eat a packed lunch in the shade of the hedge. Lord slept with his arms folded behind his head and his face turned up to the sky.

'I suppose so,' said Ellie.

'Is there anything to stop us going? No one seems to check on us. No one seems to take a blind bit of notice what we do.'

'Well?' she said.

'I could just keep walking towards the Estates until I knew where I was.'

She had picked a flower from under the hedge and was pulling the petals with such deliberateness that it irritated him and he turned away from her.

'And then?' she asked.

'I'd go home.'

'And then?' When he didn't answer she reached out and touched him lightly and kindly on the shoulder, repeating, 'And then? What, when you got home?'

'They wouldn't know who I was.'

'There's no going back. Get that out of your head. Ask Lord,' she said, instinctively lowering her voice, although Lord slept on undisturbed by them. 'He went back once. Before my time. He wasn't Lord then, but Binder or Hook even. He was young and fed up with it. But he was back within a month, half-starved. He won't ever tell what happened, but he'll tell you he was back within the month and glad his place wasn't taken.'

'Didn't they know he was gone?'

'Not they,' she said scornfully. 'They're on the Drink, you know, and there's a different lot in every dome. The Reapers come and then they go and the Guardians forget all about them until the time comes round for harvesting again. They count them at the beginning of the harvest and again at the end. So long as five come and five go, they're not really bothered. You don't exist once you're here, not so far as they're concerned.'

'But if they counted, they must have know there was a man short.'

'Someone must have stood in for him. He'd have fixed that to give himself time to get clear.'

'Who?'

'I never asked. Someone that cared enough to want to help him, though there was little enough in it for them. Perhaps the woman I took over from. I never ask about that.'

'Are you married to Lord?'

'In a manner of speaking.'

'Did you choose him?'

'Goodness no. I was just sent to fill in a gap. We all are.'

'Was I?'

'Yes,' she said. 'The old Binder took sick. He wasn't any good really. Never took to the work. Hook became Binder. Lad became Hook. You became Lad.'

'Is it always like that?'

'Yes, always.'

'Don't you mind?'

'Mind what?'

'Not choosing.'

'It's funny really,' said Ellie. 'I've made a right muck up of choosing. Sharon's father and Mandy's and Kevin's, each as bad as each other. All went off in the end. He's far and away the best man I've been with, and I'd no say in it at all. Funny, isn't it?'

'I should like to choose,' he said. It occurred to him that he should like at least to keep his name, to feel that Sharon, for instance, kept hers, had some choice as to whom she lived with and what she did. He knew suddenly that he would not stay. A little longer perhaps. He had a feeling that there was still something to be done. But after that he'd go, not back to the Estates, but following, perhaps, the ghostly track westwards beyond the domes to where there were no buildings, only a world made up of the gaps between them.

'You'll come with me, Paul?' Ellie said when they reached the Eastern domes. 'I feel quite choked at seeing her again.'

They left Lord to inspect the crops and, asking directions from a passing band of Sowers, set out for the Home for Recalcitrant Old Ladies. It lay beyond the settlement, another half hour's walk away, set in a fold of the southern slope of the downs, a fine stone house with pillars flanking the entrance and a clutter of sheds and huts built up around it. Inside, the defiant odour of disinfectant was strong. Nurses in green overalls over their workmen's clothes wheeled the crouched old ladies briskly down corridors covered in black linoleum. When they asked for Sharon they were directed to the rose garden.

Roses sprawled over the low stone walls and the sunken paving. The warm afternoon air was sweet with their scent. They found Sharon sitting on a stone bench at the side of a fishpond staring dreamily down at the fish. Beside her, an ancient lady dozed in a chair.

'Hello, Mum,' she said when she heard her name. Her face was as unmoved as if she had expected them.

'Hello, Sharon.'

'Feeling better?'

'Ever so much better.'

'The kids are OK.'

'Kevin?' said Ellie Willmay eagerly. 'Kevin?'

'Yes, Mum. He looked real well.'

'And happy?'

'Yes. Really happy.'

'And Mandy?'

'Her too.'

'She'd find it easier.'

'Ellie Willmay,' said a scratched peremptory voice. 'Why don't you speak to me?'

Paul glanced around the empty garden before he associated the voice with the old woman. Ellie bent over and looked into the fierce cloud-coloured eyes that stared up into hers.

'Gran,' she said aghast. 'I thought you were dead.'

'Well, that's a nice greeting after all these years. Nine years in this hole come Midsummer and not one of you's found time to visit me until Sharon here. She's a good girl, Sharon. Always was. You were always too hard on her, Ellie.'

'Now, Gran, you know we couldn't come.'

'Well, what's past is past,' said the old lady sulkily, but a moment later something like a smile spread the deep wrinkles puckering her mouth. 'Just like the substandards up Ravensbury, eh, Ellie? All together again. Remember the substandards up Ravensbury, Sharon?'

'Yes,' said Sharon, who had begun to cry.

'Those were the days, before our troubles began.'

'It was like one big happy family there,' said Ellie. 'Neighbours and all. You could ask anything of anyone.'

'Not like the Ackroyden,' said Sharon.

'Stuck-up place, the Ackroyden,' said her mum. 'Except for Jeanie. Jeanie was all right.'

'Only I never could abide your husband, Ellie. He spoilt things, most days. Whatever happened to him?'

Ellie shrugged. 'What I wouldn't give for a ciggy,' she said.

'A cup of coffee, eh, Ellie? We must have drunk six in the day up Ravensbury. You weren't too badly off then. Who's he?' she said, suddenly aware of Paul.

'He's a friend, Gran.'

But the old lady continued to glower suspiciously at Paul, whom it seemed she had confused with Ellie's former husband.

'Let me take her for a walk,' Ellie said to Sharon. 'You talk to Paul.'

When they were alone, Sharon smiled at him. 'It is Paul, isn't it?'

'You always knew me before.'

'But you've changed. You don't know how you've changed.' But she continued to smile in a way that made him feel the change must be acceptable. She had changed too. Her face was fuller. He thought she looked happier. The sun had rubbed colour into her cheeks that seemed to reflect light up into her eyes. She asked him about his life as a Reaper and he told her about her mother and Lord. 'It's odd, isn't it?' he said. 'Us all meeting up again like this.'

'Not really. Not when you come to think of it.'

But he was distracted from wondering what she might mean by breaking off a rose for her, by noticing how its colours intensified in the deep convolutions at its centre, by the sweetness of the humming air, by supposing that she felt as he did that their meeting again was inevitable and entirely right.

'Do you want to stay here?' he asked her when her head was bent, fitting the pink rose into the top pocket of her overall.

'No, not really.'

'What about your mum?'

'She's got Gran back – and this man she likes.'

'And the little ones?'

'There's no getting them back.'

'What about going on then? Before they allot you to some bloke. Before it's too late. With me.'

'I'd like that.'

Late in the afternoon, Lord arrived at the Home to collect them. Ellie introduced him to Sharon and the old lady. He had been given the contract for Midsummer Day and was able to promise them both to bring Ellie back with him on Midsummer's Eve. The Reapers would have to camp overnight in order to make an early start on the harvest the following morning. Sharon said she had that day off and would come and help her mother with the cooking.

'It was nice seeing Sharon again, wasn't it?' said Ellie as they began the walk home.

'Yes,' said Paul, who wondered now that he had thought so little about her in the past weeks.

The road was very dusty. It rose ahead of them to the crest of a slight rise that seemed to support the entire sky. They climbed in silence, hearing, as they approached the top, voices on the other side. Then, over the hill appeared a small party of people laughing and talking among themselves. The cloud of dust they raised shimmered about their brightly coloured clothes. The women's gay skirts fluttered at their knees. Even the men wore coloured ribbons around their odd flat-topped straw hats, and tight pink and red roses in their button holes. Two young men swung a large hamper between them. They seemed to Paul to be not entirely real, but it was impossible to doubt, from the liveliness of their conversation and their obvious pleasure, their reality to one another.

As soon as they saw the three drab figures approaching, they lowered their voices and turned their smiles defensively outwards. Ellie, Lord and Paul had moved to the side of the road. The strangely dressed people seemed greatly obliged. The older man – *the father*, thought Paul – called out, 'A good evening to you,' and lifted his hat, revealing a startlingly pale skin and a pouched, lugubrious face.

It was Dr Palmer.

But even as Paul's face livened with recognition, Dr Palmer's eyes fell quickly, but blankly, upon him, and then glided on. Ellie, too, he did not seem to know. (*Have I changed as much as she has?* thought Paul.) But he called out, 'Wilson, isn't it? Lord, I suppose I should say. A very good evening to you, Lord.'

'The same to you, sir,' said Lord, who had pulled off his hat, but spoke distantly as if out of obligation.

'You're far from home, aren't you, Lord?'

'Have to go where the work is, sir. We've contracted for Number Three on Midsummer Day.'

'Have you now? Conditions about right?'

'Excellent. I'd say ideal, sir.'

Once more the quick bright eyes flickered towards Paul as if a trace of recognition stirred, but no, he looked away and moved on. The others trooped smiling at his heels. One of the women, in a pretty blue and white flowered dress, he thought for a moment was the nurse who had given him the books for Ellie, but he could not be sure. Nor did she know him. All the women and the two youths wore the dull placid stare of the uncontaminated.

'We'll meet on Midsummer Day then, in the harvest field,' said Dr Palmer.

'In the harvest field, sir,' replied Lord. It was as if he had taken up a challenge.

CHAPTER SEVENTEEN

On the day before the Reapers set out for the Midsummer harvest, Paul told Lord that he intended to leave directly it was over and try his fortunes in the West.

He had wondered if Lord might persuade him to stay, but he simply said, 'If you're going, you shouldn't leave it any later in the year than this.'

'Will it leave you short-handed?'

'We'll give you a month,' said Lord. 'Then we'll report you missing. They'll replace you off the Estates. We can manage that long.'

'What if they notice I'm not here.'

'If they don't happen upon the fact in the first three days, they won't know you ever existed. That's not your problem. Your problem's making a go of it. Getting settled in somewhere and getting a supply of food over the winter.

There's plenty has set out West and not come back. They can't all be dead, although I daresay one or two are. If you stick to that track we were on yesterday you're sure to come to a settlement sooner or later that will take you in.'

Paul had the impression that Lord had taken the same journey often enough in imagination, but always at the last held back from it. The others, too, seemed excited by his venture as if it awakened in them old longings for freedom and movement. At the same time he felt they were relieved it was he and not they that was setting out in search of these things. As if in gratitude they each brought him gifts – Binder, Hook and Lady – small sacks of seed saved out of their vegetable garden for just such a journey should they ever take it. It was too late to plant now, but they told him any settlement he came to would be pleased to barter for seed from outside. Only a little must be kept back for himself for the following spring.

Lord gave him a knife. Ellie, from her store of clothing, found him two thick sweaters and two pairs of heavy socks, and returned to him the weatherproof jacket he had worn on the Estates. She sat on the edge of his bed, watching as he packed all these treasures carefully into his rucksack.

'Are you taking Sharon with you?'

'Yes, if she'll come.'

'Whatever will become of you?'

'We'll be all right. You'll see. We'll get word to you where we are.'

She brightened up then. 'We'll come and join you some day, Lord and I. When Gran dies,' she added, pushing the decision out of the foreseeable future.

He smiled at her. 'We'll be all right.'

The Reapers walked to the Eastern domes late that afternoon, wheeling a handcart along the bumpy track in which were stacked the tents and Ellie's cooking pans. Paul wore his rucksack to accustom himself to the weight of it. They set up their camp just off the track in sight of the domes. By the time that Sharon had finished work and come out to join them, the tents were pitched, a fire lit in a little grate and a thick vegetable stew bubbled in the pan. Paul noticed that she, too, carried a rucksack, but he made no attempt to ask her what she intended. He kept apart from her and watched her face alter in the firelight as she stirred the stew.

The others, too, kept off the subject of his journey. It seemed wisest to wait and see what tomorrow held. He had the same knowledge that had disturbed him before the first harvest, that some event lay between him and the future, cutting him off from it. There was something still to be enacted before he was free to go.

Lord roused them all before dawn. They struck camp in a dim grey light thrown up from below the high horizon by a sun not yet visible. When the tents were packed in the cart they grouped around the fire for breakfast. The sky was lightening, taking on colour. Birds in the hedges began to sing. As they set out for the domes, the sun rose before their faces.

Lord led the way to the dome he had inspected on his last visit. There, in expectation of their arrival, a little knot of Guardians stood at ease across the path. As they came nearer they could see among them the tall figure of the real Lord.

He was dressed in breeches and a checked jacket. Leather boots shone round the swelling of his calves but were powdered with dust at his feet. A cloth cap was tilted forward over his eyes so that he raised his head and looked down the bridge of his long nose at the Guardians he talked to. Apparently the talk was pleasant. The Guardians' deferential laughter caught occasionally in the microphones on their visors and blared out, shrill and demonic. The sound made Paul shiver. The sun could not warm him.

Newly risen in a nimbus of pink, it quivered and balanced on the apex of the glowing dome, seeming one substance with it. Paul feasted his eyes on it, but in his heart suddenly he remembered the Estates and winter; the strips of grey sky lowered over the straight streets, the discarded plastic bags by the walls and railings whispering insanely, driven into wild contortions by the wind, the caged trees rattling against their bars. Things which had no meaning in his new life were realities again. The controlling presence of Dr Palmer put the world at risk. Winter was inevitable.

Panic battered and fluttered in his head and in his chest, desperate for release. He stared at the sun until sun and dome disintegrated into flakes of brightly coloured light.

Around him he was half aware of the ritual of the contract being enacted, not away in a hut this time, but in the open. In front of the formation of Guardians drawn up across the path, Dr Palmer bargained for their hire with Lord. The Reapers stood a little to one side, watching from under the straw brims of their hats. The psychiatrist, tolerant and amused, jutted out his chin to look down below the peak of his cap on Lord who repeated in his slow controlled voice, his complement of men, the area of the dome, the time that would be taken, the cost that would be involved. Paul watched in Dr Palmer the need to appear generous before the Guardians without appearing a fool before the Reapers.

'Four men, you say. Four men and a Lad.' His eyes, shaded by his cap, were directed towards Paul, moved on, hesitated, returned, paused, moved away. *He knows*, thought Paul. *Not yet by name, but he knows that he knows me. He will not let it rest.*

There was no more time. Necessity took hold of him. His mind cleared. The plan rested in it, ready made. He moved behind Hook and Binder, and taking the straw hat from his head handed it quickly to Sharon.

'Will you wear it?' he whispered. 'Will you wear it into the field for me?' There was no time to think what he asked her. Her eyes widened a little with apprehension, but she said simply, 'Yes.' Dr Palmer was naming his price – higher than normal, but not ridiculously so. By way of explanation he made a gracious reference to the time of year, to Lord's reputation as leading the best team in the field. The Guardians turned towards him and began politely to clap their gauntleted hands. No one noticed the swift movement with which Sharon scraped her hair into the crown of the hat and pulled it down over her eyes, nor Paul as he withdrew to the back of the little group of Reapers.

Dr Palmer's head was bent as he groped in his pocket for the silver coins of the Midsummer bounty. Paul moved as quickly as a cloud on the sun to the wall of the hut. He waited there with his heart pounding, but the Guardians, blinkered by their helmets, intent on the ceremony, had contented themselves with counting the figures to whom Lord distributed the shillings. So too, it appeared, had Dr Palmer whom Paul feared more than they. He edged his way around the wall of the hut until he came to the red tap handle that worked the irrigation system. He rested his hands upon it. He had no idea how much force was needed to turn it. He dared not try yet lest the Guardians who surveyed the inside of the dome be alerted. He stood quite still, listening to the familiar sounds of the ceremony and judging from them the exact position of the Reapers.

There was the mindless force of the Guardians' chant,

'*Left, right, left, right.*' The rattle of the iron bar raising. The whine of the great doors on their semicircular track. '*Left, right, left, right,*' and again the whine and then the rattle.

He recognised Dr Palmer's voice, blurred and magnified by a loud hailer: 'I put it out to you.' The answer was inaudible, but then, as though through a great distance in time, he heard the lament of the Reapers from inside the dome, '*Oah! Oah! Oah!*' His hands tightened on the metal rim of the wheel. Then he heard the triumphant release of their sorrow, '*Ahhhhh.*' He flung his weight against the tap handle, counted to three, and began to turn.

What am I doing to them? he thought in terror. Their lament echoed in his head above the vicious ripping sound that issued from the dome as the simulated rain and the simulated lightning flash combined.

A scream made enormous by a microphone destroyed all other sounds. Microphones began to babble. The loudhailer boomed among them. He leant on the wheel, sick at heart at what he had felt compelled to do. Until, from inside the dome, he heard a faint defiant cheer.

He ran out then, careless of being seen. The skin of the dome blazed near its top, sending flames shooting to the sun, feeding it strength against the winter he had feared – so that his heart rejoiced. From inside the dome he heard the Reapers raise cheer upon cheer. The flames shrank rapidly downward. The substance of the skin was so inflammable that it was consumed as soon as it flared, and brilliant flakes of fire that floated free of it vanished before they reached the ground.

The ring of fire grew as it worked rapidly down the dome. The black skeleton of the framework rose unharmed above it. The irrigation system continued to play, but the flames spread outwards and downwards with such speed that they escaped quenching.

Inside, he could see the Reapers standing among the corn with their faces turned up to the rain, waving their hats and cheering. The blaze was over within minutes. As soon as it reached the concrete base of the dome and came into contact with the waterproof seal that cemented the two substances, it let out an evil smell and a dense cloud of smoke. This was his only chance. He began to run towards the dome, blinded and choked by the smoke. He jumped over the base of the dome, burying his face in his hands. He was blundering among the corn. His eyes began to clear. He managed to call out Sharon's name.

She was running towards him, her fair hair flattened and darkened by the artificial rain, holding out his hat in her hand. As she reached the circle of smoke, she hesitated.

'Go on!' he shouted to her desperately. 'Quick, while they can't see you.'

She ran past him then, holding out his hat. He snatched it from her and waited to see her leap into the smoke and vanish from sight. Then he flung himself forward and began to force his way between the stiff stalks on hands and knees, towards the knot of Reapers who had fled to the centre of the field.

'Paul Simonds,' blared Dr Palmer's voice. 'I know who you are and that you have caused this fire. I know that you are hiding in the cornfield. If you come out quietly, now, I shall do my best to help you. If you resist, the Guardians will be sent in after you.'

Paul knelt and pulled the hat down over his eyes. The smoke was thinning, but he could still only guess at Dr Palmer's position from his voice. He rose quickly to his feet beside the Reapers, just as Lord shouted back, 'Begging your pardon, sir, but that won't be so easy.'

'How's that?' came from the hailer. Paul could see the psychiatrist now, hailer in hand, the Guardians grouped around him, standing at a little distance from the dome.

'We've taken the contract, sir. The field itself is undamaged. The contract still stands.'

'So?'

'So no one enters the field, sir, until we cut the corn. It's as simple as that. Those are our terms and we stand by them.'

In an instant his words were backed by the deadly rattle of the blades on whetstones of his fellow Reapers.

'This is absurd,' shouted Dr Palmer. 'You are harbouring a dangerous criminal in there who might have burnt you all alive.'

'That's not so, sir. He knew well enough what the domes were made of and how they would behave. He's done us no harm.'

'He's one of you, you mean.'

'That I could not say, sir, not knowing the name you called him by. We've our own names here, and our own laws, which are well known to you. You know well enough, sir, that no real Lord would be safe setting foot on the harvest field, and the same is true of your Guardians. They are strangers to us and not welcome here until our task is done.'

Dr Palmer had come to the very edge of the field now, with his Guardians grouped behind him. He made as if to move forward, but instantly Lord shouted, 'This will never do, sir.'

The circle of Reapers formed. The deadly whirr of stone and blade sounded.

'*Holla Lar*,' shouted Lord. '*Holla Lar. Holla Largess.*'

And the long sad cry answered him, '*Oah! Oah! Oah!*' to the mounting rattle of blades.

The Guardians could have picked them off one by one and laid them in the corn, but the ancient ways prevailed. Dr Palmer was the real Lord. The fear that drove him back was the real fear. The Guardians parted to let him pass, and regrouped behind him. From his original position he raised the loudhailer to his lips and shouted, 'Very well then. We'll leave you to do our work for us. The field is surrounded.

Anyone hiding there will be discovered by you. When the last corn is cut the field is mine again. We know how many entered the field. If you try to leave it with an extra man amongst you, you all share in his punishment.'

While he was still speaking, a van drove at high speed up to the dome and more Guardians poured from it through the cloud of dust that they had risen. They began to jog along the smouldering perimeter of the dome, taking up positions at regular intervals. Dr Palmer turned on his heel and walked back to the van. He was, Paul remembered, too busy a man to stand arguing by the side of a corn field. He climbed aboard. The engine roared forward. Dust rose from under the wheels. He was gone.

'Now to it, boys,' said Lord calmly. 'We've wasted enough time.'

It was the best and most memorable of harvests. The sun beat directly on Paul's back and burnt along his arms. The corn had come alive, swaying and sighing in the warm June wind as if a spirit moved among it. He worked in the corn as if he were a part of it, an agent of the sun, bringing the harvest to completion. His blade flashed like its rays. Rising to stretch his back, he shaded his eyes to watch the corn spirit flee across the rippling stalks ahead of him. Then he bent again in pursuit of it.

They ate their brief meal in rapt silence, not retiring to the edge of the field where the Guardians kept up their vigilance, but staying close to the standing corn. Now they worked in a ring around it, enclosing the last of it. 'Easy, Lad,' warned Lord. 'Best they see you come last.'

Paul stood over the last of the corn where the hunted spirit crouched, where he, Paul, lay hidden. He heard for the last time the cry:

'*What havee? What havee? What havee?*' He raised his face to the sky where no barrier lay between himself and the first glittering star, and shouted into its depths:

'*A neck! A neck! A neck!*' and struck all dead with a blow.

They bound him in straw then, arranging it to hide his face, and carried him, unhindered, from the field. They were counted and dismissed. The ring of Guardians moved inward, crunching across the stubble field in their futile search.

Out of sight of the dome, they set Paul on his feet and helped him strip off the straw. Ahead of him on the path, Sharon waited with the rucksacks, ready to leave on the long walk towards the sun which hesitated for them on the western horizon.

But Lord took his arm and, turning him slightly, pointed to the east where the next cluster of domes was just visible. As they watched, there was a flare of light. Flames shot briefly from the surface of one dome, then another, then another.

'You're not alone, Lad,' said Lord. 'There'll be others travelling with you.' And even while he spoke, they saw another fire appear, further eastwards still, blazing up on the darkening hills.

To find out more about *The Vandal*,
as well as discover other exciting books, visit:

www.catnippublishing.co.uk